Quartet  Qrime

VARIATION ON A THEME

Also by David E. Fisher

The Man You Sleep With

DAVID E. FISHER

Variation on a Theme

QUARTET QRIME

All of the characters in this book are fictitious,
and any resemblance to actual persons, living or dead,
is purely coincidental.

First published in Great Britain by Quartet Books Limited 1982
A member of the Namara Group
27/29 Goodge Street, London W1P 1FD

First published in the United States of America
by Doubleday & Company, Inc. 1981

Copyright © 1981 by David E. Fisher

British Library Cataloguing in Publication Data

Fisher, David
Variation on a theme.
I. Title
823'.914[F]   PR6056.I/

ISBN 0-7043-2349-4

Printed and bound in Great Britain
by Mackays of Chatham Ltd, Kent

For Leila:
Here's looking at you, kid

VARIATION ON A THEME

CHAPTER 1

The thing is, I don't like to play the idiot. The sucker. I don't like to be taken advantage of. More than most people, I mean. Because I'm vulnerable.

For example, I never count my change in the supermarket. I go to the supermarket, buy a six-pack of Beck's Dark, maybe a quarter pound of Nova, a nice chunk of Jarlsberg, a decent steak, and some flour to bake a loaf of bread, I give the cashier a twenty, and I figure there's not going to be enough change to bother counting it, right? So if she wants to cheat me I'm vulnerable.

Okay, that's a decision I've made. I don't want to walk through life looking in my pockets every time someone bumps me, to see if he picked my pocket. I don't want to be always looking over my shoulder. Like Satchel says, something may be gaining on you.

So I've made this conscious decision to trust people; it's the core of my philosophy. Trust people and they won't cheat you.

The only trouble with that is, when someone does cheat me I tend to lose my temper. More than most people.

For example, if someone murdered his wife and used *you* as his alibi, wouldn't you be just a little angry?

I was madder than hell.

If he was someone like practically your best friend, and if his wife was maybe not exactly your secret love but anyhow someone you'd at least sort of loved a long time ago, wouldn't you be angry?

I mean, I was the *fall guy*. I was this son of a bitch's *alibi!*

And I was the only one who knew he had killed her.

And then, to make things worse, they send over this *pizzella*.

It was about three days later, and I was in my apartment back in the city, West Eighty-first Street, walking up and down, bouncing off the walls, wondering what I could do about it, who should I talk to, when the phone rang. It was the Suffolk County sheriff's office, they had finally got around to assigning a detective to the case, and would I be available to give a statement?

"Sure," I said. "Where do I go?"

Don't bother, the sheriff's office said, they'd send the detective in to see me if I'd be home this afternoon. I said I'd be home this afternoon.

So just after four the buzzer rings and I jab the button and a few minutes later there's a knock on the door and I open it and there's this little *pizzella* standing there looking up at me.

I looked over her head out into the hall, but there was nobody else there.

She sighed. "Suffolk County sheriff's office," she said. "Karen Douglass." She held out her identification.

"Come on in," I said, and shut the door behind her. I led her down the long hall to the living room and we sat down. I asked her if she'd like a drink and she said a Coke and I got up again and got her the Coke and a beer for me. I brought them in and sat down again and mentioned that I had told her office I'd have been willing to go out there.

"So much of our business is city people," she said, a little nastily I thought, "that we're used to coming in for one thing or another." She smiled, as if to say she hadn't *meant* to be nasty, and I had to grin back at her. She had a cute smile.

But I was still a little aggravated. "If I had gone out to your office," I said, "I'd have been able to talk to the detective in charge of the case. Yeah, I know," I said when she started to interrupt, "I'm sure you'll write down exactly what I tell you, but it's not the same thing, you know? Words get twisted when you tell him what I tell you, it can't be helped. It would have been better if I could have talked directly to him."

"To who?"

"To whom. The detective in charge of the case. Because it's not just a question of the facts, of where I was and where he was and what time everything happened. It's this feeling I have, I'm not sure I can express it, I know goddamn well I can't express it through some secretary's notes."

The trouble was, I was still angry about being played for a sucker by my practically best friend, so I was taking it out on this *pizzella*. I knew it, and right away I felt sorry. "I'm sorry," I said. "We'll do the best we can, right? Not your fault they sent you. Ours not to reason why, right? Ours but to do or die."

"And die."

"What?"

"And die. 'Theirs not to reason why, theirs but to do and die.'"

I looked at her. I nodded. She was getting even for that *To whom* crack. She was entitled. Still, no sense letting her get a swelled head over it. Let her know who's boss right from the start, we'd get on better that way. "You that are young," I told her, "consider not the capacities of us that are old; you do measure the heat of our livers with the bitterness of your galls."

She stared at me.

A rather long silence.

I sipped my beer. You shouldn't sip beer, you should slug it down, but somehow the moment seemed to call for sipping.

She stared at me.

"Falstaff?" she asked.

She was a smart one.

I nodded.

"But you've done something to it," she complained.

"Poetic license," I said, a little irritated. "Let's get on with it. You have a notebook or something?"

"I really think we ought to get this straight, first," she said, handing her identification to me again.

"I saw it," I said.

"You didn't read it."

I took it from her. I read it.

Jesus Christ. I looked up over her card at her. "Detective?" I asked. "Really and truly?"

"Really and truly," she assured me.

I handed her wallet back to her. "You're not actually . . ."

She nodded. "I've been put in charge of this case."

"Oh, great."

"What's that supposed to mean?"

I had never actually seen hackles rise before, but hers sure as hell did. Right in front of me.

"Nothing," I said. "Just a last dying remnant of male chauvinism. Surely I'm entitled to that?"

She tried to hide a satisfied little smile. "Let's get on with it, then, shall we? Just for the record, you are Mr.

Henry Grace of West Eighty-first Street, New York City? Forty-two years old. Occupation, playwright. Currently unemployed."

"My play *The Courtesy Not to Bleed* is now running at the Gotham Guild," I told her, not too pompously.

She glanced at her notes. "You are not being paid for the privilege," she said.

I shrugged. That's show biz.

"Currently unemployed," she decided. "Now then, tell me about this murder most foul."

"It's not easy," I said.

"I know," she said. "It never is."

And I had to laugh. She lifted a quizzical eyebrow, but I wasn't about to tell her why I had laughed. It was the way she sat there, notebook open and ready, pencil poised, and the way she said, "I know, it never is." So right. So—hell, just so perfect. *I know how it is, I understand, I empathize, it never is easy, everyone has this problem, just take it easy and recount the events to the best of your recollection....*

The parfit policeperson. Just like they must have taught her in school. Polite, sympathetic, professional.

But I was damned if I was going to tell her why I had laughed.

"I don't know where to start," I said.

"Start at the beginning," she said.

Oh, Christ. I sighed. And I wasn't going to tell her why I sighed, either.

"Do you want the facts," I asked, "or the truth?"

She didn't even pause to blink. "First the facts," she said. "The truth comes later."

Did they teach her stuff like that in school, too? Or was there actually a brain inside that head? A very cute little head, by the way. Black hair, straight but soft, it sort of fell around her face in a way that framed it. Big eyes, dark brown. Very trim little body. Sitting erect, poised, waiting for me to begin.

"It's a long story," I warned her. "I can't just start with the murder."

"Begin—"

"At the beginning. Right. Here goes, then."

It was a long time ago. It was yesterday. I could nearly reach out and touch it. But not quite. A star at the corner of your eye, tantalizing, twinkling, but turn your head and look directly at it and it's gone. It was nearly twenty years ago. It was 1962.

Nineteen sixty-two. Summertime. The Bellport Gateway Theatre, just beyond Patchogue, seventy miles out on Long Island. Empty country and summer houses. Westhampton and beyond that Montauk. Nineteen sixty-two.

I was an actor then. Actually, just beginning to realize that I wasn't an actor; unable to comprehend the fact, unable to blink it away. I *must* be an actor, I told myself, I must be a pretty damned good actor, how else could I have got this job? Summer stock, repertory, five plays in eight weeks, beginning with the Sewer King in *Madwoman*, a great part, I could play all over the stage in this one.

Turner was stage manager. He was more mature than I, same age but more mature. He was facing up to it sooner, looking for something else to do with his life. What do you do when you quit school to tread the boards, and then the boards are no longer willing to lie there and be trod by you? Become a brain surgeon? A nuclear physicist? A Howdy-Doody Ice Cream Man?

Turner got the job stage-managing at the Bellport, I don't know how. But they're always desperate for a good stage manager: desperate enough, I guess, to take anyone who was willing to claim experience.

"They just asked me if I had any background in s.m.," Turner told me. He grinned wickedly. "I said, sure." He spread his hands dramatically and shrugged. "How was I to know they meant stage-managing?"

Then once he got the job he had a say in the hiring of the company, and that's how I got taken on. It's not what you know in this goddamn business, it's who. Which is a bloody shame, isn't it? Still, when it's offered, you have to grab it with both hands and hold on as tightly as you can.

In those days it was all a lark. It was all "There's No Business Like Show Business" and "Another Openin', Another Show" and on to Frisco, Philly, or Baltimo', and out to Bellport, Long Island.

Where we met Sarah.

I know what everyone thinks about summer stock companies. I've sat in enough bars after the performance and had people creep up shyly to say they had just seen us in the show and it was so great, they really loved it, and we ought to be on Broadway, and all the time they're standing there looking out of the corner of their eyes at the little ingenues in the tight slacks and the loose blouses, I've sat in enough bars and murmured kind words to enough people like that and seen the look in their eyes often enough to know what everyone thinks about these summer stock companies, all right.

The bohemian life.

That's what they think it is. They've all heard about actresses, especially the nubile young things in summer stock. They've seen the Judy Garland movies and they know what the Hays Office made them leave out, they know what's really going on. They're convinced of it, I've seen it in their eyes a hundred times as they look wistfully at a gang of us sitting around an *après* show pizza at the local boozery. They just know it, that we're all sleeping together.

What can I tell you? They're right.

There's a lot wrong with this business—there's no security, and it's all run according to the Golden Rule: "Them as has the gold makes the rules," and tryouts are degrading and call-backs will drive a strong man to drink— there's an awful lot wrong with this silly business, but the camaraderie is real and the sex is very good indeed.

The first week of summer stock everyone pairs off. Sometimes the pairing is permanent—they last all summer —and sometimes it isn't. But anyhow, that first week everyone looks around, tries to get together, sort out the sleeping arrangements.

So right away that first week we paired off, Sarah and I. And Turner.

The little detective glanced up. She caught me looking at her in that sexy way I have, and she glanced right back down again. She kept on writing in her notebook.

"Well, hell," I explained. "We were young then. You remember when you were young, don't you, Detective? You remember how it was."

I wasn't sure if she was embarrassed or acting snotty. So I turned away and walked over to the window to look out, then suddenly turned back and caught her looking at me. As I turned, her eyes went right back down to the notebook. But I caught the look in them. It was embarrassed.

Which was fine. Embarrassed is much better than snotty. Especially at her age. I waited.

She waited.

Hell, I could wait all day. She was the one that had to get things moving again.

Finally she said, "Lieutenant."

"What?"

"The proper form of address is Lieutenant, not Detective. Detective is a description, not a title."

So she was still in there fighting.

I didn't have a cigarette, so I couldn't dangle it out of the corner of my mouth and squint through the smoke, but I tried it anyway. I squinted and flicked my lips and said, "How'd a sweet dish like you get in a crummy racket like this, sweetheart?"

"It's a long story, Sam," she said, "and we've got work to do," nodding to her notebook. "Let's get on with it, shall we?"

It wasn't anything depraved. It wasn't even especially sensational. I mean, it would never have made the front page of the *National Enquirer*. Nothing like that.

Not at first.

At first, it was just Sarah and I together. Smiling quickly across the stage at each other when the leading lady made an ass of herself during the first rehearsals. Patting each other's bottom as we passed while moving the scenery into place—it was supposed to be Equity, which means the *artistes* don't empty the garbage, but get out beyond Patchogue and you're in God's own country where nobody knows "City" rules. Flicking paint at each other as we strolled to get the flats hung in time for opening.

That sort of thing. Beer and pizza after rehearsal, coffee together in the morning. Nothing very special. Sleeping together, of course.

The fun started the third Monday night.

Now you're asking yourself how, nearly twenty years later, how do I know it was the third Monday night?

Well, to be honest, I don't know. I mean, I'm not one hundred percent sure, but it was definitely a Monday night. I know that because we were dark on Mondays.

So Turner and I and a few close comrades had a poker game going on Mondays. That was one of the things we did whenever we worked together. No women. A real poker game, like the good old days you read about.

Now, this particular poker night—I think it was just about the third one of that summer—Turner wasn't doing too well. Which wasn't all that unusual. Now, ordinarily, your classy poker game might go on all night, but this particular night it was only ten-thirty when Turner stood up, yawned, stretched, and said, "I guess that finishes me."

I looked up at him. What was the man talking about? I remember I was pulling in a pot at the time.

"That cleans me out," he said. "I'll have to drop."

"What are you talking about?"

"I'm a little short this week," he said. "I can't hang in there with you Mississippi riverboat gamblers."

I pushed a stack of chips over to him. "I'll stake you to five," I said, not thinking anything about it.

"No, it's not my night," he said. "I better just drop."

"I'm winning," I told him. "I can loan you the bread."

"You'd be betting against your own money," he said. "That's no way to play poker. I'm not in the mood anyway. Never mind. I'll just cut out."

"Hang around and kibbitz, then."

"No, I don't think so. *Ciao*, all."

He sounded just a little embarrassed. I mean, I didn't think so at the time, I didn't notice anything. But afterward, thinking back on it, I could see where he had been just a little embarrassed.

No wonder.

I was shuffling at that moment. I gave the deck the old magic riffle and said something casual, like "See you tomorrow, then," and glanced up at him as I said it and the cards went spraying out of my hands and spilled all over the table.

Now, you have to understand this. You have to believe me. There's no way I can explain it simply, it's not just cut and dried.

But I'd known Turner for two, maybe three years by that time. We had met at tryouts for *Threepenny Opera* way back when, and we had both been turned down, so we had a lot to talk about. We got along together right from the beginning. We were both new in New York, we didn't know anybody.

I mean, for a couple of years I *knew* him, really knew him. Like when he would say something about how Brando had sold out to the movies, I knew that what he meant was he'd give his right arm for just one of Brando's used-up old sparks. When we'd go see Olivier do *Henry V* for the tenth time and we'd come walking out of the theater and he'd say, "How does that limey son of a bitch get away with crap like that?" I knew what he meant: that if Olivier offered either of us a chance to work with him which involved having our throats ripped open onstage by a pack of ravenous rats, we'd have jumped at it.

We understood each other.

And so that night when he threw his cards down on the table and stood up and said he was going to cut out early, and I was sitting there shuffling the cards, I wasn't thinking anything special about it. Until I happened to glance up at him.

And then I saw it.

I saw it in the way he was standing, his weight just a little bit more on the left leg than the right, his hips just a little bit twisted and forward, his hands resting lightly on his belt.

I saw the look on his face and the casual slouch, the way he stood there for a moment before he turned and went to the door.

I saw it and, goddamn it, I knew immediately.

He was going to Sarah.

She wasn't writing any of this down.

"You don't think it's important?" I asked her. "You think Sarah was killed by a burglar, an itinerant psycho, and Turner and I—our relationships with each other, Turner and Sarah and I—just aren't important?"

"I didn't say that," she said.

"You're not writing any of it down."

"I don't see what you're getting at. I don't understand the general plot. Until I do, I can't know what's important. I don't know what to write down. Just keep talking. Tell me the whole story. I'm listening. When you've finished, I'll know what's important."

Turner never said anything to me. He never actually said, "I'm sleeping with Sarah," or anything like that. But he knew that I knew, and I knew that he knew that I knew.

At the beginning of a show I'd generally be working later each evening than he did; after the rehearsal ended and his job was done there would usually be a group of us getting together to work informally on a particular scene. Since he wasn't involved with anything like that, he'd be free. So he'd go see Sarah while I was still working. By the time I finished work and came back to her place, he'd be gone.

Later on, in the final days of rehearsal or when a show had actually opened, the situation would be reversed. Rehearsal or performance would be over and I'd be finished, but he'd still have to hang around a couple of hours cleaning up, getting things set for the next day, making sure Props and Scenery were on the ball. On those nights I'd see her first.

I don't really know if she thought she was fooling either of us. But one night—it was a tech rehearsal for *Three Angels*, I think, and Turner was going to be there half the night—after Sarah and I had taken our pleasure of each other and I had fallen asleep for half an hour, I got up and got dressed and, still half asleep, as I was pulling on my moccasins I remembered that I had borrowed an Agatha Christie from Turner. It was one that he had taken out of the Bellport Library and it was due the next day. Turner would be up late tonight with the tech rehearsal, and he'd want to sleep late in the morning.

So I said to Sarah, without thinking, "Tell Turner I'll return the Agatha Christie for him in the morning."

And then I realized what I had said. I glanced up at her, and she realized it too. She stared at me for a long second, then gave a horrified little giggle and turned over and buried her face in the pillow.

What could I say? I patted her on her bare rump and left.

Well, Pangloss was right. At least after that it was all out in the open. Much better that way. Without more ado our two twosomes became one threesome. We hung out together, had our beer and pizza together—one pizza is too much for two people anyway; it's just right for three, I'm surprised more people haven't thought of that. At any rate, it was probably about a week later that one night after the beer and pizza she came back to our place and came to my bed and then went openly across the bare wooden floor to his.

The next day we went into Patchogue and bought a secondhand double-bed mattress and dragged it back and pushed the two twins together and threw the mattress over the both of them. The three of us slept together the rest of that summer.

She still kept her own apartment, for appearance' sake. Her parents lived out on the North Shore near Port Jeff. They didn't know anything about this kind of larking around, and probably wouldn't have appreciated it.

The three of us would go over there for dinner maybe once a week. They knew we were all close friends, but that's as far as it went. I wonder if they ever wondered if their daughter was sleeping with one of us? I wonder which one they suspected.

A couple of times, on dark nights, we spent the night. They had a nice place, right on the Sound, with enough rooms so that we each had our own. Sarah, during the night, would creep from one of us to the other, like the yellow fog on little cat feet.

But time and tide wait for no man, and helter-skelter, willy-nilly, life tears along on its reckless pace from day to day, right? And so we come to the end of that summer of 1962.

We come to the end of it one glorious August afternoon on the sands of Westhampton Beach, Turner, Sarah, and I. I knew something had been bothering Turner, but I wasn't sure what. He had been kind of moody the last few days. Well, I guess I *did* know what. It was the same old thing. The end of the season, the end of a job. And who knew when or from where the next job would be coming?

A new season looming empty and long in front of us, with nothing definite in sight except an unemployment check for twenty-six weeks.

It was always a depressing time. Nothing new about that.

I was lying on my back, my eyes closed, storing up the sun in preparation for the cold winter to come. Turner and Sarah were lying next to me.

And then out of nowhere came Turner's voice: "I guess you'll have to marry one of us one of these days, huh?"

I didn't open my eyes. We had all been skating around the question of any sort of permanent relationship, skating very delicately indeed. None of us had discussed what we were going to do when the season closed.

"I guess I will," Sarah said.

Again a long silence. The surf came booming in below us. The sun kept beating down. Some sea gulls were screeching a ways down the beach.

"Which one?" Turner asked.

Again the silence. The surf, the sand. The sea gulls.

"You, I suppose," she said finally. "Unless Henry minds."

I opened my eyes. I glanced over at them. They were just lying there, not touching, not looking at each other. Sarah's eyes were closed, her face turned to the sun. Turner was looking at me.

It was that same look on his face. He wanted her, and he had won.

But there was a little bit more there. I could read it as clearly as if it had been part of the program notes. There was a little bit of fear there. He hadn't quite won. "Unless Henry minds," she had said.

And if Henry *did* mind?

The question hung there on his face.

I lay back down again, closed my eyes to the sun.
"I don't mind," I said.

"*Did* you mind?" the little detective asked.

"I don't know. I guess yes, some. But not too much. Not enough to screw things up for Turner. I guess what I really wanted was for things to go on the way they were, for us to go back to the city and move in together. But then it turned out that that wasn't what they had in mind at all."

"What did they have in mind?"

I don't know what impression I gave you, but I have to tell you the truth. Which is that onstage we were not all that great. Turner and Sarah and I. In bed together we were something else. But onstage, collectively and singly, we weren't exactly the Lunts. Not even half a Lunt among the three of us.

So it was more than just a long, dull season out of work that loomed ahead of us. It was the rest of our long, dull, empty lives.

I was already thinking of trying to write a play. I wasn't talking about it yet, I didn't have the chutzpah to talk out loud about myself as a writer. I hadn't yet touched pencil to paper. But after a season out in stock on the Island anybody with an ounce of brains has to begin thinking that he can write better dialogue than the crap we fed those audiences.

Turner and Sarah, it turned out, had something else in mind. I've mentioned that we went to visit her folks about once a week all that summer. Her father ran a real estate agency on the North Shore. Mostly summer rentals, that kind of stuff.

Well, we'd go there for a meal, spend the evening, and

he'd pour us a couple of beers and talk about how the Island was all set to explode population-wise. That's literally the way he talked. Real estate agent talk.

And I guess I never heard it because I wasn't listening for it, but apparently he was throwing out hints. And Turner was fielding them as fast as he could throw them.

And so the season ended, and I gave Sarah one last slap and tickle and kissed her good-bye and packed my bag and headed back in to the city on the goddamned Long Island Rail Road for another winter of discontent. And Turner stayed on Long Island with Sarah and her parents.

And the real estate agency.

Sarah had never been serious about the profession, and I wasn't surprised that she was quitting. She had tried it because she was young and pretty and wanted her fling, but she had enough sense to realize that she wasn't really an actress. When she outgrew her ingenue roles there would be nothing left for her; and when a young lass's only talents are the bloom in her cheeks and the line of her legs, she outgrows those roles very quickly indeed.

I was surprised at Turner, though.

I suppose I shouldn't have been. His taking the stage manager position that summer instead of looking for an acting job certainly signified the end of his ambitions onstage. And during that summer he had become pally with the business manager and that whole group. He made no secret of it, he wasn't even ashamed. He said he found the business aspect fascinating.

And, of course, once you make the jump from acting to business, you'd be a chump not to take the much smaller jump from the business of acting to the business of business. There's no business like show business primarily because other businesses show a profit.

Sarah's father was the real estate baron of Miller Place, Long Island. Which doesn't sound like much to us big-city boys, but it was a situation with a future. Her father assured us.

He was just sitting out there on the Island waiting for the city to fill up and overflow and spread its tentacles farther and farther east. Sooner or later, he told us all that summer, those tentacles were going to devour every acre closer in to the city and would be reaching the seventy miles all the way out to Miller Place. And what would those tentacles find when they got there? They would find him, he told us, just sitting there rocking on his front porch with every property in town sewn up tight.

And sitting just as pretty, he hinted as gently as Sherman marched through Georgia, would be his heir. Whoever that might be, he used to say, glancing from one of us to the other and avoiding his daughter's eyes.

And so Turner was seduced.

And so I left him.

With many fond protestations, of course, protestations of seeing each other frequently and not losing touch. With promises of comps to all my Broadway openings, and assurances on his part of finding me the best summer home on the North Shore as soon as I was ready to plunk down a few hundred casual grand.

And so, oblivion.

I went back to the city on the Long Island Rail Road and descended the nine levels of hell. At that time, the season following that summer, if I had been successful I would have kept in touch. I would have dropped them a postcard to say I'd been cast in an Off-Broadway revue, I would have called them long distance to mention casually that Kazan had signed me for the new Tennessee Williams. . . .

But I wasn't going to stay in touch only to complain, to have them commiserate, to have them suggest that I might want to join them in the joys of Island life. And so, oblivion.

Finally, late that winter, I was jobbed in to a Wisconsin rep. I thought that was the nadir of my life. I left the city as if to exile, expecting never to return. I would live the rest of my life in Wisconsin, in Indiana, in Ohio or Wyoming. I would grow old, I would grow old, I would wear the bottoms of my trousers rolled. It never for a moment crossed my mind to tell Turner and Sarah.

But it turned out rather well after all. I discovered that the best actors and the best plays in this country are not necessarily in New York, that it's quite possible to do good work out in the boondocks. But I also discovered that it's not possible to *live* out in the boondocks. You can rent a place, and eat, and breathe, but there isn't much living to be done in Wisconsin. Unless you're into hunting and fishing and other blood sports.

Out of self-defense, to keep my sanity, I began to write.

Fade out. Music up and over. Fade in.

Act Two. Years later.

Nearly twenty years later. By this time I am no longer acting. I have had three plays produced along the national repertory circuit. They bring me in a few dollars. A very few dollars. I have also written four thriller novels. They bring in a bit more. With one thing and another, I survive. And two or three times a year there's that sudden surge of excitement when the phone rings late at night and it's Los Angeles calling, some bankrupt producer who wants to know if the movie rights to one or another of them are still available. And I answer yes, and I sit by the phone day and night without moving, without daring to get up to go to the bathroom for the next three weeks for fear that I'll miss the call-back, I sit there waiting for that damned phone to ring again, until finally the pressure from my bladder overcomes the pressure between my ears. And the phone never rings again.

And then just a few months ago my latest play, *The Courtesy Not to Bleed*, was picked up by the Gotham Guild for production here in New York.

The Gotham Guild pays *bubkes*. It's officially an Off-Off-Broadway house, but it's getting known as a showcase. Several of its plays the last couple of years have moved on to Broadway, and one play produced there and you're set for life. Especially if you've developed inexpensive tastes from years of knocking around the rep circuit. So I accepted their offer gratefully.

They pay a bare subsistence wage during production, but I found a cheap sublet through a friend who was off for a few months making spaghetti Westerns. And so I settled back into life in the Big City.

The rehearsal process was hell. The director turned out to have a completely different idea of what the play was about than I did, so we had to fight about it for four weeks. But finally we got it onstage, and it opened and the reviews were pretty good. Pretty damned good. Probably not good enough to move it on to Broadway, although we haven't completely given up hope. But they've certainly generated interest for the next play I'm working on. So life was beginning to perk up.

I hadn't even thought of contacting Turner and Sarah. It had been nearly twenty years and I had grown into a different life. I never thought of them, any more than you do of your high school friends.

And then suddenly, after a performance one night, I came through the backstage door into the lobby and there she was.

Sarah.

And oh, Christ, it was just like in the movies! I came in through the door leading from what they laughingly call backstage directly into what they hysterically call the lobby, and she was standing there. Her back was to me, but I recognized her immediately. Which means something, I guess. I hadn't consciously thought of her for years, but the moment I caught sight of the back of her head, there it all was flaring up inside all over again.

She turned then and saw me, and for just one moment we stood there staring at each other. And then we took one step toward each other, two steps, three steps, and then we were running across the small lobby just like in the movies, leaping into each other's arms.

We needed someplace to sit and talk. A bar wouldn't have been right at all. We walked down the street looking for a coffee shop, but nothing was open at that hour. It soon got too cold to look anymore.

"I've got a place just off Broadway," I said.

She smiled and nodded, her face bundled and humped down into her upturned collar, and we hurried down the street.

She was quiet while I made coffee. I was thinking frantically of what to say to her. There were no words, none at all. We'd made small talk as we hurried through the cold streets, and all the time we were both aware how silly it had sounded.

Now she stood and waited silently while I made the coffee. I dragged it out as long as I could, but finally there was nothing left to do. I dried my hands slowly and turned around and looked at her and there was only one thing on both our minds and both of us knew it but I didn't have the guts to say it.

She did.

"I want you," she said.

Simply. Just like that.

And then again, "Oh, Christ, I do want you!"

"The coffee—" I began.

She reached out and pulled the plug.

I reached out and took her hand and led her into the bedroom.

"You sure you don't want to write any of this down?" I asked her.

"When you've finished, we'll review it and I'll write everything down then."

I wasn't quite convinced. "It's all important," I assured her. "I'm not just coming on with you, you know."

"That never crossed my mind. You're so obviously not my type. And I'm sure that, since you're a playwright, you have the sensibility to realize that. So let's get on with it, shall we?"

Wow. Talk about being put down by an expert.

I nodded, but I didn't go on. I just sat there looking at her. Then I asked, I don't know why, "What's your name?"

"My name?"

"I don't even know your name," I said.

"I told you to read my identification. Believe it or not, my name's on it."

"Nobody ever reads those things. What's the point? You can buy them in the five and ten."

She almost smiled, decided against it, and sighed instead. "Karen Douglass," she said. "Two esses."

"Karen Douglass. Two esses. Right."

The room was stuffy with unadjustable heat and we were both wet with sweat, although we could hear the cold wind outside still howling. Her long blond hair was hanging down all over my face. She lifted herself on her elbows and swung her head from side to side, brushing the tips of that lovely blond hair back and forth across my face.

I must have dozed off and she must have got up and finished making the coffee. I was lying in bed, half sitting up, holding a cup. Sarah was next to me, sharing the propped-up pillows, holding her own cup in both hands. Well, I guess she had to. She had given me the cup with the handle.

"Here's looking at you, kid," I toasted her, sipping the coffee. Terrible coffee.

"Bung ho," she said. "Who always used to say 'Bung ho'?"

"Lady Brett."

"You think you're so great. I need help."

She threw that in so casually that I didn't hear her at first. I went on sipping the terrible coffee and her words just floated around until finally I heard them.

"Help?" I asked.

She nodded, not looking at me, staring into her cup. She looked so frail, holding the handleless cup with both hands.

"What kind of help?"

She didn't answer right away. Finally she asked, "You won't leave me again?"

Christ, there it was. Twenty years too late. "You're married," I said.

"And I need help."

"I wouldn't be any help. I'd only make it worse."

She looked at me then. "You don't know what it is that's wrong."

"Okay, what is it that's wrong?"

"I don't know," she whispered.

It sounds stupid, but what can I tell you? All I know is that the way she said it, I just melted. "I'll help you," I said. "Tell me what's wrong."

"I really *don't* know. Come visit us, come be our friend again. Turner needs you. He's changed. He's so different."

"How do you mean, different?"

"I don't know. He frightens me sometimes."

I didn't understand that. I said so.

"Sometimes he looks at me—when he doesn't know I see him. I might be reading or knitting or watching TV, and then if I suddenly turn and catch him staring at me— I don't know how to explain it. I'm frightened."

I said, "That's silly."

"Maybe it is," she agreed eagerly. "Maybe it *is* silly. I'm just imagining things! I'm sure that's all it is, but I can't *help* it."

And you know, *that* scared me. She was so eager to believe that she was being silly, imagining things. That scared me, because if you really are imagining things that's the last thing you want to be told.

"What could I do to help?" I asked.

"Come visit us? Just come and *be* with us. It was so good when the three of us were together. Come out to visit us?"

She smiled a little smile. It's not easy to smile shyly when you're lying in bed naked with a guy and the sheet's down around your hips, but she did it. She smiled shyly, frightened that I'd say no.

I reached over and took the cup out of her hands gently, placed it down on the floor beside the bed. I put my arms around her and she folded into them and I held her like that, gently, quietly, until she wasn't afraid anymore.

I guess I went into a kind of reverie thinking about all that, thinking about Sarah lying there safe and warm because now she was in my arms again, and thinking of her lying cold and dead and splashed in her own blood on the floor of her house where Turner and I had found her—

I went into a kind of reverie and came out of it suddenly and didn't know where I was. I looked up and there across the room was the little *pizzella* detective sitting on the couch, and for just one moment in the gloom of that winter afternoon with the heavy shadows crossing the room and falling over her face I thought it was Sarah. Christ, for that one moment I swear I could smell the salt air of the North Shore instead of the monoxide of the city, for that one moment I was back out on the Island and Sarah was alive and I was just waking up from a nightmare—

But then she moved, and no wild strands of long blond hair shifted around her head. She had short, straight, dark hair and she wasn't Sarah and it wasn't a nightmare I had been dreaming—it was a nightmare I was waking up to, it was real.

Sarah had asked me for help. She had come to me and told me she was afraid, that Turner was going to kill her, and I had thought she was playing boy-girl games, I had laughed at her, I had sent her back to Turner, and he had killed her.

"Are you all right?" the *pizzella* asked.

I nodded. "Just thinking what a prick I am. Sorry."

"You're thinking you should have helped her?"

I nodded.

"How?" she asked.

"Christ, I don't know! I should at least have listened to her. What *could* I have done? I don't know."

"Tell me what happened."

"She had her teeth pulled."

"Her teeth?"

"Her wisdom teeth. It must be in the report, the coroner's report! Christ, didn't you even read it?"

"I didn't notice that. Is it important?"

"Yes."

"How? What does having her teeth pulled have to do with being murdered?"

I was quiet. "I don't know," I had to say. I took a deep breath. I didn't know. I don't know how he did it. But looking back now, it seems—I don't know, maybe I'm wrong—but it seems like that's what set it all in motion. Sarah saying that she had to have her wisdom teeth pulled.

"Come stay with us," she asked. "I'll need you particularly this weekend."

"What's so special about the weekend?"

"My damned wisdom teeth are coming out on Friday."

"I didn't know that," Turner said.

We were all sitting in what they called the parlor. We'd been out for a lobster dinner and had had a few beers, and now we were back in their house sitting lazily around in the last hours of the night. Just three old friends, sitting around quietly.

One of us terribly frightened. Not knowing why.

"I went back to that bloody dentist yesterday and he said all four of them have to come out. He says it's easier to do them all at once."

"Will he give you an anesthetic?" Turner asked.

"Oh yes."

"And we'll get you some codeine or sleeping tablets for afterward," Turner said. "You'll be all right."

She glanced at me. She didn't want to be alone in the

house with Turner and with her blood full of codeine and sleeping pills.

I had been up there to see them about four times in the last few weeks. I very nearly hadn't gone at all. I very nearly packed my stuff and ran off. That night—the first night, when I met Sarah in the lobby of the theater—after she left that night to drive back out to the Island and to Turner, I lay awake a long time. Thinking about things. About Sarah. About Sarah and Turner and me.

About how I had felt at the end of that twenty-year-gone summer when she had left me to marry him. I guess it had bothered me more than I'd let on. I guess I'd been pretty miserable there for a while.

I didn't like to think about it now. It had been a hard time.

So now the question was, did I want to start that up again? There was no question in my mind of trying to take her away from Turner; I would never do that. So if we started up again, what it would lead to was either a good friendship with the two of them, or a sneaky romance with Sarah whenever Turner turned his back. Possibly both, but more likely the latter.

It was four-thirty in the morning. It was raining outside. An ambulance was tearing up Amsterdam. And I was miserable and alone and I decided Christ no, I do not want that. I cannot take all that again, I'm too old, too damned bloody old for that kind of stuff.

And I rolled over and tried to sleep. And I kept seeing her face. Scared.

And I kept hearing her voice.

"I'm frightened. I don't know why. . . . He frightens me. . . ."

And so the next morning when the phone rang and it was Turner, what could I tell him? I heard him tell me how Sarah had told him that she'd bumped into me and how well I looked and how happy we all were and when was I going to come on out there and tell him about life on the wicked stage?

So a few days later I walked down the street in the rain that never stopped and took the Long Island Rail Road from Penn Station out to Long Island, to Sarah and Turner and whatever the hell was going on out there.

I got up and took another beer.

"Did your relationship continue?" she asked. "During the three or four times you said you visited them."

"Sure. That was what she was after, wasn't it?"

"I don't know. Was it?"

"Christ, lady, *I* don't know! How long have you been a detective? Aren't you supposed to know all about the vagaries of human conduct? The passion, the pain, and the sweet sweet love?"

"Tell me about the sleeping pills," she said. "Turner suggested them?"

"Yes. It seemed like a good idea."

"And Sarah asked you to stay with her for the weekend?"

"Yes."

"And you did?"

"Well, I didn't stay with her the whole weekend, did I? By Saturday night she was dead."

About eight o'clock Saturday night. The three of us are in the parlor. We have just finished dinner. Steak for Turner and me, oatmeal for Sarah. Her cheeks are swollen, her face is flushed, her eyes are nearly shut. She is wearing her blue bathrobe. Turner is reading the local paper. I am wishing I was back in Wisconsin.

"Hey, look at this!" Turner says.

Sarah lifts one drooping eyelid, then drops it closed again. I lift one eyebrow, Errol Flynn style. We are not too excited.

But Turner is. "Guess what's playing at the university? *Gunga Din!*"

I perked up at that. Just about any movie would have been preferable to staying in that night, and *Gunga Din* is preferable to just about any movie on just about any night.

"What's that?" Sarah asked.

Turner glanced at me. He smiled. I commiserated. "You probably wouldn't like it," he said. "It's a movie about tribal warfare on the Northwest Frontier. Victor McLaglen—"

The idiot. That was the wrong way to talk her into going to see it. So I quickly interpolated, "And Cary Grant."

"Cary Grant? When was it made?"

"Late thirties."

"Cary Grant in the late thirties?" It was remarkable how quickly she was recovering. She sat up and swung her legs down and tried to stand—and then fell back onto the couch.

"Oh shit," she said delicately.

Turner had been feeding her codeine all day. She was in no shape to get up and go out.

"You two go," she said.

We made polite demurring noises, but she said she meant it, she was ready to go to bed anyhow, and Turner said she could take a couple of sleeping pills and she'd certainly sleep till we got back, and I made a couple of half-hearted protests but I was really dying to see *Gunga*

Din again, and in the end she took the pills and Turner and I went out.

The movie was being shown at the university, about fifteen miles away. The performance started at nine o'clock, so we left her at maybe eight-thirty. Turner took her up to bed and gave her the sleeping pills, and then I went up and said good night while he got the car out of the garage.

So I was the last person to see her. Falling asleep in her bed, the blue bathrobe folded over the chair, her long blond hair falling over the pillow.

We saw the movie and came straight home afterward. The show broke just a little before eleven; we were probably pulling into the driveway at a quarter past. Turner drove right into the garage. We got out of the car, he closed the garage doors from the inside, he opened the door leading from the garage into the house and gestured me in.

I went in, he followed.

So I was the first one to see her.

The garage door leads directly into Turner's den. It's a dark little room, lined with bookshelves, lit only by a desk lamp.

The lamp was lit, casting a small circle of light.

In front of the desk, on the floor, lay Sarah.

I saw her, and couldn't move.

"What's wrong?" Turner bumped into me as I stopped short.

I pointed.

She was in the blue bathrobe, her blond hair spilling all around her head and spreading out on the dark brown carpet.

Turner jumped in front of me, kneeled down beside

her, then groaned and fell backwards against me. We sort of pulled each other out of the room.

"Her throat's been cut," he gasped. He started to heave, and I was afraid he was going to vomit all over me. But he swallowed it down. He was green, his mouth was open, he was gasping for air. He held on to me tightly. I thought he might faint. I thought *I* might faint, and I hadn't seen her up close.

"Is she—"

"She's dead."

"Are you sure? Maybe—"

"Her throat's been ripped in half! You want to see it? You want to go look at it?"

I shook my head. No, I didn't want to see that.

"She's cold," he said. "Like ice. Like death. We have to call the police!" he said suddenly.

"Yes, of course, the police." I wasn't thinking. I couldn't think. I was terrified, I didn't know what to do. I guess it was a mild case of shock. It didn't feel mild, though.

It's not too clear, I have to admit. But the next thing I knew we were in the hallway and Turner was dialing the phone, then jiggling it and dialing again, and then he said, "It's no use. Oh, God, look at that, the phone wire's been ripped out."

And then we talked about what to do and we decided we'd have to go in the car to get the cops. It's very deserted out there, you know, in the winter. It's a summer resort town, hardly anybody really lives there all year. We didn't see lights in any houses.

So we went out to the garage and got in the car, and then Turner said he couldn't leave her alone like that and I should go without him. I was so flummoxed by then I wouldn't have argued with anybody. I got in the car and drove across the island to Patchogue, to the state troopers' office. That was the first police station we knew about. It was about half an hour from when I left that we got back.

Then the cops took over and now you know everything I know, and that's not much.

Because neither of us knows how that son of a bitch managed to kill her.

"Not quite everything," she said.

I was torn up all over again going through the story, and I didn't hear her at first. She had to repeat it.

"I don't know quite everything you know," she said, "because I don't know how you know that he *did* kill her."

I nodded. "Right." How could I tell her? How could I explain it? "You remember," I began, "that poker game I told you about? That night he left me playing poker to go to her?"

"I remember."

"And I knew right away what was happening. No one else did, no one else thought anything about it. But I saw that look of triumph on his face. *He had won.* And he wanted me to know it! I guess that isn't proof, is it?"

"Proof of what?" the little detective asked.

"I guess I couldn't stand up in court and say '*J'accuse*' on the basis of one look, could I?"

"I don't know what you're talking about."

"Later, after the cops had gone, is what I'm talking about. After we had told them everything and they had taken Sarah's body away and had dusted for fingerprints and had found the ripped telephone wire and the broken glass in the den where the intruder must have come in and even found his footprints on the damp grass out in the yard and where he had carried mud into the den.

Later, when they had all gone, when we came back into the house and locked the doors, he turned to me and asked if I wanted a drink or anything, and *right then* I saw it again!"

"Saw what?" she asked, but she knew.

I nodded, knowing that she knew. "The look," I whispered. "That same damned look. And he wanted me to see it!

"Because he had won. And so he wanted me to know that *somehow* he had killed her, he wanted me to know that he knew I knew that, and he knew that I'd never know how, I'd never be able to prove it, there wasn't a damned thing I could do about it."

CHAPTER 2

A month passed and nothing happened. I expected at first to hear from the *pizzella* any day with news of what she had found out when they investigated further, dug into Turner's background, searched the house, done whatever. When people murder people they have to leave fingerprints in the wrong places, or footprints, or a flake of dust from an unused quarry or *something*, right?

But the days passed, the weeks passed, a month passed and I didn't notice it. I had troubles of my own. My new play had been optioned after all for a Broadway production, which I thought when I signed the contract meant I was set for life. It's a small cast, one set, and should come in at minimum cost, so even a so-so success would mean a fortune. And then there would be productions forever in colleges and little theaters and regional reps, and the money just keeps coming in for the rest of your life. That's what I thought it meant when I signed the contract.

What it actually meant was that the only way I could avoid a nervous breakdown was to hold tight and grow an ulcer instead. The producer suggested—this was maybe three or four days after I had talked to the *pizzella*, Karen Douglass—he suggested Paul Newman might want to star in my play and direct it, both on Broadway and in the movie. What did I think of that suggestion, he wanted to know.

So of course I slobbered all over him. And he went out and called up Paul Newman right away. Only Paul Newman wasn't home. So he wrote him a letter. Then he wrote his agent a letter. Then another one. Then he suggested maybe Elia Kazan would be a better director.

"What's wrong with Paul Newman?" I asked.

"What's wrong with Elia?"

Well, nothing's wrong with Elia Kazan. But what happened to Paul Newman? God knows, but a couple of weeks later whatever had happened to him happened to Elia Kazan, too. "What do you think of Alan Schneider?" he asked.

"What happened to Elia Kazan?" I asked.

Producers are very good at not answering this type of question. You can ask as often as you like, and rephrase it as deftly as you like, but if you ask a question they don't want to answer they will talk as long as you like and just never answer. They're very good at that.

They're also good at cutting their losses. The terms of the option agreement state that I'm to receive three hundred dollars a month until rehearsals begin, and then—it doesn't matter what then. Because yesterday I got a short note informing me that under the terms of the agreement the option was being dropped and there would be no further payments of any kind. And, of course, no Broadway production.

"What happened?" I asked my agent.

Agents can shrug over the phone. I don't know how they do it. "Newman didn't want to do it," he said. "Kazan didn't want to do it, even Schneider—"

"There are ten million directors in this city looking for work—" I began to scream. But agents are good at not listening. That's their profession, really. That and picking their noses. I stopped screaming. "What happened?" I asked.

"What can I tell you?"

Nothing. I already knew whatever he could have told me. Because of the unions it would cost over two hundred thousand to put on even a small-cast, one-set production. That's a lot of money for a show that Paul Newman doesn't like, that Elia Kazan doesn't like, that even Alan Schneider doesn't like. . . .

So I was left with a run-out option and an active ulcer. I couldn't blame the producer, or even Paul Newman. So instead I splurged on a long-distance call to Suffolk County, to Karen Douglass, girl detective.

She sounded like my agent. *What can I tell you*, etc.? They had found footprints leading from the garden to the french doors, glass from the broken door on the inside of the house, grass and dirt on the carpeting. There was no grass or dirt on Turner's shoes. The footprints in the garden were from a different type of shoe, a size and a half larger than Turner's. They had found indications of a car parked around the side of the house, tire tracks on the swale. Okay, maybe someone just happened to be passing by and for some reason pulled over and stopped. Maybe. But at this time of year it's a deserted neighborhood. So all the evidence was consistent with a burglar, a forced entry, a smash and grab that went awry.

"It doesn't prove a forced entry," I suggested. "It's all circumstantial."

"Nothing ever proves anything," she told me. "All proof is circumstantial, unless you have a witness. Actually we do have a witness, but before we go into that may I remind you of Ockham's razor?"

"No. Tell me about the witness."

"Ockham's razor is a principle first enunciated by the fourteenth-century philosopher William of Ockham—"

"I hate college girls," I said. "I bet it was a girls' college. Smith? Wellesley?"

"Brandeis," she said. "Ockham's razor tells us that quote entities are not to be multiplied unnecessarily unquote."

Silence.

I thought.

Then I said, "I can do you one better. Ontogeny recapitulates phylogeny."

"What's that got to do with solving crimes?"

"What's Ockham's razor got to do with solving crimes? With Turner murdering Sarah?"

"It means that hypotheses should not be piled on and on and on, it means you should stick to the simplest possible solution of the available evidence. It means when all you have is circumstantial evidence, the best solution is the simplest. In this case, forced entry."

"There are all kinds of possibilities—"

"But no evidence of them. We couldn't find any indication that Turner had a reason to murder his wife, nothing out of line turned up in their marriage—"

"I told you Sarah was worried about him, she didn't understand him. . . ."

I don't know much about marriage, but even to me that didn't sound terribly unusual. Then I suddenly remembered what she had said before she started distracting me with Ockham's razor. "Tell me about the witness," I said. "You said you had a witness. Who is it?"

"You," she said. "Remember?"

Shit. Hoist on my own petard.

"You were the last one to see Sarah alive. You were with Turner every minute from then until you found her dead. To tell you the truth, if we gave up the idea of a forced entry—our number one suspect wouldn't be Turner. It would be you."

After she hung up I glared at the phone. Then I glared at the wall. I walked over to the window and glared at the dust inside and the dirt outside. I hated New York City, Long Island, Karen Douglass, and the horse she rode in on. I hated Broadway and my ulcer and the bloody Ayatollah. And Paul Newman in spades.

Which only made it more delightful the next morning when the photographs came.

CHAPTER 3

I took the LIRR out to Patchogue, and then got a cab to her office. She suggested we talk over lunch, and I was afraid we'd have to take another cab. Cab fares out on the Island are astronomical, and I no longer had the expectation of a million dollars coming in from my play.

But never fear, we walked out the back door to the parking lot and got into her car. Nothing ostentatious, only a Jaguar XKE sedan. Such is life in the suburbs.

We went to a place on the North Shore called the Wagon Wheel. Rustic on the outside, Versailles on the inside. She said she liked it because they served such lovely drinks. She ordered one by the name of maracaibo orange delicious. It came in a coconut, with a straw. I asked if they had Beck's Dark beer. They didn't. I ordered a Budweiser.

I wasn't going to let all this spoil my delight. I thought of the photographs in my pocket, picked up my beer, gestured with it toward her, and said—

She interrupted. "Let me say it," she said. She lifted her own drink, clinked it against my beer, and said, "Here's looking at you, kid."

I winced.

"That is what you were going to say, isn't it?" she asked.

I nodded, reluctantly. "It seemed appropriate," I told

her. "I feel like I'm playing private detective. Sam Spade, Philip Marlowe, whoever."

"This is a business visit, then? I suppose I shouldn't be drinking."

"You're not," I told her. "That isn't a drink."

She smiled. "And this isn't business, it's an obsession. I told you there's nothing more we can do, unless you manage to come up with some evidence."

"Right, lady," I said. I took out the package of photographs without taking my steely blue eyes off her face, peeled off the top one, and slid it across the table at her. "Do you recognize this man?"

She looked down at it while I looked at her, waiting for a reaction. There wasn't one. She looked at it for a moment, then asked, "Do I recognize this man? Are you being funny?"

She slid it back across the table to me. I looked down at it. It showed a naked girl on her knees before a naked man. The man was shown only from the waist down.

"Wrong picture," I muttered. I looked through the other pictures and picked out a good one. This one showed the man on top of the girl. It caught him clearly in profile. His face, I mean. I handed it to her.

She recognized him right away. "It's Turner, all right. Where did you get this?"

I handed her all the pictures. They were Polaroid snaps, showing Turner and this girl and another guy. Mostly Turner and the girl or this other guy and the girl, but one had all three of them in it. That one wasn't quite in focus; they had obviously positioned the camera on the floor and used a self-timer.

She looked at each of them in turn, spreading them out on the table in front of her. "Where did you get them?" she asked again.

"Yesterday's mail. Anonymously."

The waitress came to take our food order. Detective Douglass ordered Dover sole. The waitress didn't seem to hear. She was leaning over as far as she could without actually seeming to, looking at the pictures spread out on the table. I didn't know how I was going to pay for Dover sole on my salary, which at the moment was nonexistent, but I said, "Make it two," kicked the waitress on the shin, repeated our order, finally got it through to her, and reluctantly she left us.

The *pizzella* looked at me. "It's not proof of murder," she said. "It's not even against the law."

"Not against the law?" I asked. "Not even in Suffolk County? Boy, if they knew about that in the Hamptons . . ."

"There's judicial law," she said, "and there's street law. Are you suggesting we bring him in on suspicion of fornication, adultery, and perhaps sodomy?"

"What *is* sodomy?" I asked. I was interested. I'd never understood the term.

"Unnatural intercourse, according to Webster—"

"I know that. Every junior high school kid knows that. What I mean is, what do you have to do to get arrested for it? Seven will get you three it's different in Suffolk County than in the Village."

"You *can't* get arrested for it. No one's interested. Not even in Bellport. Can we talk about these"—she tapped the pictures—"in relation to our murder?"

The waitress brought the Dover soles. Karen cleared a space for the plates among the pictures.

"They're significant," I said. "They're an indication that something is rotten in the state of Denmark. They're proof that something was going on. Something that Turner didn't tell you about when you questioned him."

"I'd hardly expect him to."

"You'd hardly expect him to tell you if he murdered his wife, too. This isn't Dover sole."

"Of course not. It's local flounder. And the Roquefort dressing on the salad is really blue cheese. But fresh flounder is better than sole frozen in Dover, isn't it?"

"Principle of the thing," I muttered, thinking *principle hell, it's the goddamn price*. "The point is, everything isn't simple and aboveboard. Maybe he was in love with this girl."

She glanced at the pictures as she ate. She looked up at me. She smiled.

"Look, he was weird," I insisted. "I told you that right from the start. Who knows what was going on in his mind?"

"What do you suggest we actually do?"

"I suggest you *actually* find this girl and this guy, and talk to them about what they know about Turner, about his relationship with his wife."

"These pictures could have been taken five or ten years ago."

"They could have been, but they weren't." I looked through the stack, picked one out, and flipped it at her. "Look at that bald spot. Turner couldn't have had a bald spot five years ago, or even a couple of years ago."

She finished her sole in silence, then excused herself and left the table. I watched her walk to the rack of telephones in the rear. When she returned she said that her boss wouldn't accept a bald spot as a quantitative analysis of the date of the pictures. "Probably because he doesn't like to think about his own bald spot," she said. "Men are funny."

"So what now?"

"If you can find clear evidence that the pictures were

taken recently, it might be grounds for reopening the investigation."

I was ready for her. I flipped again through the pictures and took another one out. "Look at that. The newspaper on that chair in the background. It's the *Times*. I bet with a good magnifying glass you could read at least part of it, and then it's just a question of looking through old copies to find it. And Bob's your uncle."

"Beautiful," she agreed. "But Bob's *your* uncle."

"What does that mean?"

"It means you're the one who's going to look through old copies of the *Times*."

"Hey, this is drudgery. Routine boring police work. Don't you read McBain, Marric, Wambaugh? This is how crimes are solved."

She smiled. "Sorry. I won't be able to get permission to spend a day in the library looking through old *Times*es. It's you or no one."

I sighed. "Okay, I'll do it. I guess I have to. I'm not going to let that son of a bitch get away with this."

"Good," she said. "Then if you're finished with your sole, I'd better be getting back to work. Or should we have one more drink, for old *Times*es' sake?"

It wasn't hard after all. So much for all that crap about the drudgery of police work. It took maybe ten minutes. I bought a good magnifying glass and I could see right away it was the sports page, and with just a little squinting I could make out a line that read: ". . . and Den Herder's second sack of Todd . . ."

So it was a game between the Jets and the Dolphins. I called the *Times* sports room and they told me they had played November 16, and then they checked and said yes, Den Herder had sacked Todd twice during that game.

And this was Todd's first year at quarterback for the Jets.

I made another long-distance call out to the Island. I was dreading getting this month's phone bill. Or even this month's rent bill, come to think of that. I cursed the son of a bitch who had dropped the option on my play, and then she was on the line.

"This is the Phantom of the *Times*," I told her.

"And?" she asked.

"November the seventeenth. This season. Less than three months ago."

"Bingo," she whispered.

"Goddamn right. Doubled and redoubled in spades, to mix a metaphor."

CHAPTER 4

So it was back out to Patchogue on the bloody LIRR. Maybe I should buy a monthly ticket. At least this time she met me at the station, so I saved the cab fare to police headquarters.

We disagreed on a lot, the *pizzella* and me. For openers, I was sure that Turner had killed Sarah, while Douglass was only mildly suspicious. But she and I both agreed on the next step, and so I was waiting in the office when Turner came in and said hello and sat down.

The way I figured it was this. Turner had murdered Sarah. The thing I didn't know was how. Then all of a sudden these pictures show up in the mail. It couldn't be coincidence. I mean, why would anyone send me pictures of Turner screwing around if it didn't have some bearing on the murder? Someone knew, and wanted him caught.

The way the *pizzella* figured it, she didn't know if Turner had killed her or not. Almost certainly not, she insisted, since he had such a perfect alibi in my testimony. Which infuriated me. Anyhow, her reasoning was this: the only trail she could see in which the photos could have anything to do with murder would be if somehow Sarah had suddenly found out about them. Then there might have been a big fight and he loses his temper and kills her. Right?

But it certainly didn't happen that way. *If* he killed her, it was clearly premeditated, carefully planned. And that couldn't be, since we hadn't planned on going out that evening until the last second when he saw that *Gunga Din* was playing at the university theater. So he couldn't possibly have had anything arranged in advance. Unless . . . he *could* have known in advance about *Gunga Din*, and he would have known that it would be a pretty safe bet that I'd want to see it; I *always* want to see *Gunga Din*.

But still, he couldn't physically have killed Sarah himself because he was with me all the time. The only way the *pizzella* could figure it was if he hired someone. But how could he have done that, how do you find someone to murder your wife? The yellow pages?

It was all very confusing.

Nevertheless, we agreed on what was to be done next. Clearly the next step was to show Turner pictures of the girl and guy and ask if he knew them. If he had nothing to hide, he'd tell us who they were and Douglass could check them out and see if there was anything in their relationship that could lead to Sarah's murder. If he claimed he didn't know them, well, then we'd see.

So he walked into the office and was surprised to see me, and I stood up and we shook hands and the *pizzella* asked us to sit down—sounding very brisk and efficient and just like a real detective in the movies—and we sat down and she handed me a picture and asked, "Do you know this man?"

They had done a good job. It was the head and shoulders of the guy in the Polaroids. I looked at it closely. It had been enlarged, but hadn't lost much clarity. I shook my head. "I don't know him," I said.

I handed the picture to Turner.

He looked at it.

"What's this all about?" he asked.

"Your wife's murder," Douglass said.

"Did this man do it?" he asked. He looked up. "Is he a suspect?"

"Can you identify him?" the *pizzella* asked.

He looked at it again.

"No," he said.

Goddamn, we had him!

"No," he said again. "I don't know him."

Douglass took out another picture and handed it to me. It was the girl this time. "Do you know this woman?" she asked me.

I shook my head and handed the picture to Turner.

He didn't show any sign of anything. No nervousness, no surprise. He just said casually, "No, I don't know her either."

So now we knew something he didn't know. We knew he was lying. The next question was why. I would have liked to face him with it right away, but it was Douglass' show. She decided to let *why* wait, and go with *when*.

"Can you tell me where you were," she asked, "on November the seventeenth?"

He looked straight at her. "No," he said.

There was a long silence. Then he said, "Do you know where *you* were on November the seventeenth? Or last March the twenty-third?"

"Make it the whole week," she said. "November sixteenth to, say, the twenty-second."

He shrugged. "Don't be ridiculous. What's it got to do with Sarah, anyway?"

"Maybe I can pin it down for you," she said. "November sixteenth was a Sunday."

"Thanks a lot."

"The Jets played the Dolphins."

He thought about that. "Okay," he said. "Right, that helps. Sure, I saw that game. So I was in Miami."

"Miami?"

"That's where they played."

"You went all the way down to Miami to see a football game?"

He laughed. "Some people do, you know. But I didn't. I was down on business anyhow."

"Tell me."

He shrugged. "Nothing much to tell. I'm in real estate, right? So I'm trying to diversify. The Island's good right now, but the city's dying and when it dies the Island goes with it. Miami's the place to buy real estate now."

"Have you bought a lot?"

"Not a lot, I wouldn't say. A bit. Mostly I'm looking around. You can't just go in and buy, you have to know the market."

"Have you made many trips down there?"

"Yes. Maybe a half dozen in the past year."

"Did your wife go with you?"

He laughed. "No."

"Why not?"

"You don't know Miami. It's a good place to invest in, but you don't want to actually *go* there. Well I mean, who do you have there? Not the lower classes, maybe, but certainly the lower *middle* class of New York, right? And the Cubans? Who leaves his country and sails away in a raft, right? Not the upper classes."

"And your wife wasn't interested in visiting there with you? Not even in the middle of November?" She shivered a little at the memory of November out here on the Island.

"Sarah liked the winters out here." He turned to me. "You remember, she liked cold weather."

I nodded. She did. Which meant that he had a clear field down in Miami.

CHAPTER 5

So the days began to pass again. Trickle, trickle, morning, afternoon, evening . . .

Here I stood as the days turned into March and the snow flurries turned into day-long drizzles, here I stood looking out the dirty window at the earth slowly turning the days away.

If anyone had picked up the option to my play I would have said the hell with Turner and the *pizzella* and the inexorably slowly grinding mills of the law; I would have gone on with my own life. And you'd think someone would pick up the option, wouldn't you? You'd think if a man writes a play and a professional producer thinks it's good enough to bring to Broadway and pays out good money for the privilege, you'd think someone somewhere in the world would pick up the option, wouldn't you?

But it doesn't work that way. For every good play there's a million stupid producers and only one bright one. If you let that one get off the hook, you're going to spend the rest of your days pacing back and forth in your pad, staring out the dirty windows.

When I'm writing a play I sometimes know precisely how the second-act curtain is going to work. I have this beautiful vision, I can actually see it onstage, I can see the curtain fall, I can feel the audience pulled to their feet, cheering that moment when it all comes together. Sometimes when I am writing a play I can see that perfect second-act curtain, but I can't get there because I'm stuck on the opening lines of the second act and I haven't the faintest idea how to maneuver the characters into position so that they will inevitably say those beautiful lines that will close the act so perfectly. That's when writing a play is hell, when you're sweating blood trying to turn a sheaf of blank pages into a living play with a perfect second-act curtain. That's when playwrights envy actors.

Because all an actor has to do is sit around and wait for the phone to ring, sit around and do nothing but read *New York* magazine and do the *Times* crossword puzzle and wait for someone to put a script in his hands, and then all he has to do is read the words that someone else sweated blood to put on the page. When I'm trying to dig the words out of my brain and put them down on insolent paper in the proper order, it seems to me that that is the most glorious type of life, to have nothing to do but sit around and do the crossword puzzle and wait for the phone to ring.

But when the play is finished and in the scabrous hands of your agent, when it's making the rounds and you have nothing to do but sit at home and do that stupid crossword puzzle and wait for the phone to ring, then that's not quite so pleasant. And that unringing phone is the most refined instrument of Chinese torture.

Then I could almost sympathize with actors.

I'd learned through years of experience that the one thing you cannot do in such a situation is think about the play. You have to think about something else. Anything else.

But the only other thing I had to think about was Turner. Turner and Sarah and the guy and girl in the Polaroid snapshots, and what was happening.

What was happening? Hell, I knew what was happening. The *pizzella* had made up copies of the guy and the girl and was circulating them throughout the Suffolk County police. She had sent copies into Manhattan, and I hoped they were circulating throughout the city. She had even sent copies down to Miami. And maybe someday somebody was going to recognize the girl, and then we'd be off and running. Somebody would recognize her. Maybe.

>And here face down beneath the sun
>And here upon earth's noonward height . . .

It wouldn't be so bad if I really were face down stretched out under the sun on some beach. If I concentrated real hard, I could nearly feel the heat of the ultraviolet rays soaking into my back.

And then I looked out the window at the blowing rain in the dirty street. I shivered.

I was going crazy, that's what I was doing.

And as I stood there at the dirty window, my defenses down and my resistance in rack and ruin, Turner's face swam up before me. His face, smiling at me as it had the night of Sarah's murder, telling me that he had killed her, daring me to do something about it.

What could I do about it?

Maybe I could nudge the *pizzella* a little? At least I could find out what was going on. I picked up the phone, then dropped it back on the cradle. I was so out of it, out in left field, I didn't know what was happening. Here I was, calling her up like a little old lady in a country village calling the local constabulary to find out what news they had of the village peeping Tom. A nuisance, that's all I'd be. Something for her to laugh about with her fellow cops.

No, I knew this way lay madness. I had to do something, I had to get involved, I had to shake my rump. So I called a friend of mine who was stage-managing *Chorus Line* and talked him into two house seats for Friday night, and picked up the phone again and dialed direct out to Suffolk County—the phone bill this next month was going to cripple me; did you know you can call Alaska almost as cheaply as Patchogue?—and I asked her if she'd like to come in and share a couple of free tickets I had picked up.

So what was happening? Nothing was happening.

She came in by train and I picked her up at Penn Station. "I thought you'd drive in in that lovely Jag," I said.

"Do you know what it means to drive a Jag into the city?" she asked. "It means either you park it on a city street and God knows how much of it is still there when you come back, or you give it up to a parking garage and —have you ever seen a kid's face light up when you give him a Jag to park? I shudder when I think what they do to the poor beast's insides."

We saw the show and then I suggested Café du Midi on West Forty-sixth, but she said she knew a better bistro up in the Seventies. The Seventies. In case you're from out of town, the Seventies would cost at least double West Forty-sixth. More than that even, if it was the *East* Seventies. I had thirty-five dollars in my wallet. But what could I say? So we took a cab and of course it *was* the East Seventies and there went nearly five bucks fare and a dirty look from the driver because of the tip, but she was already out of the cab and didn't notice. We went in, and of course they knew her and we got a table right away and ordered drinks. She ordered a papaya stinger. God knew how much that would cost. I figured two-fifty at least. At *least*. And then they gave us the menu and I tried not to look at the prices.

They brought her stinger and my beer and we sipped them and I asked her, "So what do you think?"

She smiled a little apologetically. "It wasn't really very good," she said.

I wasn't surprised. "Of course not. You order a stupid drink like that, what do you expect?"

"Not the drink," she said. "I didn't know you meant the drinks. I thought you meant the show."

"You didn't like it?" I felt vaguely personally affronted. I had picked *Chorus Line* because I wanted a show she couldn't turn down, I wanted to be sure she'd come in. I mean, it's not a show I would pick for myself, but it's supposed to slay them in Des Moines. And Suffolk County.

She was still apologetic. "I saw it last year. With the original cast. It's deteriorated. But what do I know? That's what I thought, anyway."

I looked at her. I nodded. "You're right," I said. It had fallen apart. It was obvious no one cared anymore. It was a hit, it was pulling in the shekels, that's all anyone cares about on Broadway. Maybe someday I'll be like that. God willing.

"Did you like it the first time?" I asked.

She nearly blushed. "Not really. It's kind of schmaltzy, isn't it?"

She was right, absolutely right, but I was astonished to hear her saying it. "Then why'd you come in to see it?" I asked.

She looked down at the menu. I think she *was* blushing. "I wanted to," she said quietly.

And I felt like I was back in high school. I felt awkward. But kind of exhilarated. You know? You remember that feeling? It's a funny kind of feeling when you're forty-two. I didn't know what to say. So I drank some beer.

"What I really meant," I said after a while, "was what do you think's happening with our murder?"

And that's when she told me that nothing was happening, nothing was going to happen, it was all over. It was a murder committed by a transient burglar, probably from the city, and he'd never show up in the neighborhood again and they'd never catch him. The case had been put in the Open file, which meant it wasn't closed but it also wasn't going to be pursued anymore.

"How come?"

"How come? What do we have? We have clear evidence of forced entry. We have—"

"We have a husband who was screwing around three weeks before his wife is killed!"

"And a husband who has the world's most perfect alibi, am I right?"

"But he did it!"

"Says who?"

"Me!"

"And who gives him the world's most perfect alibi?"

What could I say? "Me," I said.

"So, okay. The pictures were circulated, and nothing's come in. If nothing comes in on something like that in the first few days, nothing's going to come in. The pictures are looked at by the vice squad, and they either recognize them or they don't. In this case, they didn't. No reply. So where do we go from here?"

"Nowhere."

"Right. Nowhere. Skoal." She raised her drink.

"How can you drink that crap?" I had to take out my anger on something, didn't I?

"Let me taste yours," she said.

I passed it over. It was Kirin beer. She sipped it. I could imagine how it would taste after a few mouthfuls of a papaya stinger. Evidently it did. She passed it back with a polite smile.

Conversation lagged.

The waiter asked if we wanted another drink. Quickly I said no. We ordered our food. I had *coq au vin*, the cheapest thing on the menu. She asked for frogs' legs *provençale*. I didn't want to think about the bill. Hell. I thought about it. The coq au vin was $9.95, the frogs' legs $17.95. That's $28 right there. Figure at least $4.50 for the drinks. Then tax and tip—I didn't have enough. Shit. I didn't want to think about it.

I also didn't want to think about Sarah. I wondered if the ghosts of murdered people really find no rest until their killers are found.

I didn't think that, really. I just thought about thinking about it, if you know what I mean.

Finally I said, "There has to be something we can do."

"Well, I was thinking," she said.

"What?"

"Why does she have to be a hooker?"

I looked at her and shook my head in wonder. "You really thought that she had to be a hooker?"

"I just said, why does she have to be?"

"Which really means you always thought she was. Right?"

"Didn't you? Why did you think we were looking for a hooker?"

"She could be any housewife on the Island and the guy could be her husband or her boyfriend or her cousin. You were looking for a hooker because that was the only chance we had. *If* she was one, and one of the vice squad recognized her. Right?"

"She couldn't be a housewife. Could she?"

I had to smile. "You move in different circles than I do, I guess."

"That's my whole point," she said. "You wouldn't be shocked if you found out that any of your actress friends did something like that, would you?"

"Hey, come on now, lady! It was the seventeenth century when *actress* and *whore* were synonymous."

"All I meant was," she said, looking down at her plate, "that any suburban housewife might do it, but her friends would be shocked. Because maybe it's done, but it isn't *usual*."

"It's not usual among my friends either."

"But you wouldn't be shocked."

"I'm not shocked by anything. Except papaya stingers."

"Want a sip?"

"Yuck."

The conversation died. They brought our food. Afterward we ordered two cups of *filtre*. The menu didn't list the price. Probably a buck fifty apiece. What the hell.

"You said it yourself," she said. "You move in different circles. It wouldn't be so unusual. *I* didn't say it, you did."

"What's all this leading up to?"

She leaned forward across the table. "How are we going to find the people in the pictures? We tried circulating their pictures around the police departments in the hope that they'd be recognized, but they weren't. So what can we do now? Look, maybe it *is* a housewife and her husband. But if it is, we can't find them. We couldn't publish their pictures in the paper because chances are somebody might call in and say that's my wife, but the guy in the pictures wouldn't be the husband and probably it'll turn out to have nothing to do with the murder and we'd have opened a real Pandora's box and—"

"Okay, I take your point."

"But what if she's an actress?"

Our waiter brought the *filtre*. I poured for us.

"Actresses have their pictures on file, don't they?"

I nodded. "So you could check Equity," I said.

She shook her head. "I can't. When we didn't get a positive make on the pictures—that's what we call an identification," she said.

"I know," I told her. "I read books."

"When we didn't get a positive make, my boss said that's it. We've spent too much time. The case goes into the open file. Anyhow, I can't spend any more time on it."

"So where does that leave us?"

"You could."

"I could what?"

"You could spend some time on it. You could check out the Equity files, couldn't you?"

"I'm not a cop."

"You're a playwright. Couldn't you say you're looking for a particular actress to cast your new play?"

"I don't have a new play."

"I thought—"

"The option's been dropped. That means—"

"I know what that means."

I looked at her.

"I read books," she explained.

I poured us each another cup of *filtre*, emptying the pot.

"I'm sorry about your play," she said.

I shrugged.

"Someone else will put it on," she said.

I glared.

"Still," she went on, "it doesn't really matter. I mean," she continued quickly before I could strangle her, "it wouldn't matter with Equity. They won't know you don't have a play in production. You *could* check out the pictures."

I frowned. I didn't like that at all. "It would be difficult. It would be—well, unprofessional."

"Actually," she said, "I wasn't thinking of checking with New York Equity headquarters. I was thinking of a place that's likely to be a bit more, well, as you say, unprofessional."

"What place?"

"Miami."

"Miami?"

"That's where they were, weren't they? Where they took the pictures."

"They probably went down with him."

"No," she said. "I've checked with the airlines. I checked the passenger lists on his last three flights. No names were duplicated. Which means—"

I nodded. "If these people had anything to do with Sarah's murder, they're more than a one-time knock-up. So if the same people didn't accompany him on at least a couple of trips, and they *do* have something to do with the murder, they must live in Miami."

"Right on. As they say."

"So you want me to check in Miami?"

"There *is* a theater group in Miami?"

I nodded. "One pro and a couple of semipro. I happen to know some people. I suppose I could do it. It's a long shot," I warned her.

"It's our *last* shot," she warned me. "And it's unofficial, don't forget."

"There is one problem," I said, realizing it as the waiter

placed the check delicately in front of me. "I don't think I have the cash for the fare to Miami."

"There'll be a ticket waiting for you at the airport," she said, picking up the bill.

I tried to take it back from her, but she handed it to the waiter with an American Express card. "Don't make a fuss," she said. "You're not going to be one of those macho boors?"

"Heaven forfend," I said.

CHAPTER 6

The ticket was first class, that was the first thing I noticed. If it had been tourist, I probably never would have thought to glance at the charge slip that accompanied it. It was charged on American Express to Karen Douglass, not to the cops.

I didn't like that, but then I thought, what the hell? I was beginning to get the picture. That girl had more money than she knew what to do with, so if she wanted to use a couple hundred to solve a murder that would get her a promotion, why should that bother me?

"Cocktail before dinner, sir?"

Why not? It was free. "Scotch," I said.

"Johnnie Walker or J & B?"

"Johnnie Walker Red or Black?"

"Red." She smiled apologetically.

I shrugged. Very debonair, you know. "J & B, please, on the rocks." I could get used to this life.

"Yes, sir. A double?" She smiled.

I smiled back. "Why not?" I said. Why the hell not? And how are the peasants this evening? Never mind, let them eat cake.

I began to daydream as we cruised at thirty-three thousand feet over the cold rain, I began to daydream about the rich, pretty little *pizzella* as I sipped my scotch. Maybe she had so much money to throw away she'd be interested in backing a Broadway show? There's a million and a half good unemployed directors out there, a billion and a half good unemployed actors, and at least one good unemployed playwright.

"Would you like wine with your salad, sir?"

I tell you, first class is not a bad way to travel.

"What's the salad?" I asked.

"Salade Monte Carlo Nicollet."

"Which is?"

"Well, you know, lettuce and tomato and I think some carrot—"

"What's the dressing?"

"The dressing? Oh, you know." She smiled. "It's very good. It's catered by Maxim's."

"What color is the dressing?"

"White. I can bring you one—"

"What white wine do you have?"

"Chablis."

They smile even more in first class than they do in tourist. It's very frightening. "Almadén Chablis."

"Almadén's an American wine."

"Sir?"

"Chablis is in France."

Pause. Smile. "Yes, sir. Almadén Chablis. It's very good."

"I'm sure it is." It is, actually. But I don't know, it began to be depressing. "I'll have a beer," I said.

"Yes, sir. Budweiser or Miller—"

I held up my hand to stop her. "I don't want to know," I said.

What I wanted to do was sink my chin into my folded hands and close my eyes till they were only steely squints and peer through a cloud of tobacco smoke like Sherlock Holmes and figure this whole thing out.

Big chance. First of all, I was in the no-smoking section. By choice, of course. It bugs me to see corporations getting rich selling cancer. Second of all, the more I thought about it, the more I realized I didn't know anything. I didn't know *how* Turner had killed her and I didn't know *why* he had killed her.

At least I was ahead of the Suffolk County cops. They didn't even know *if* he had killed her.

Never mind. First things first. What I didn't know *first* was who had sent me the dirty pictures. And why.

I settled down in my wide seat to think about that, and I think I had just about fallen asleep when she woke me to bring my salad and beer.

They poured me off the airplane after three more beers with dinner and a cognac with Irish coffee—well, I couldn't refuse all that, could I? I couldn't resist it. So I staggered through Miami International Airport and into a cab. I flopped down in the backseat and closed my eyes, thankful that they had focused well enough to get me this far, and said, "Players Theatre, please."

"*Qué?*"

I opened my eyes. The driver had turned around in his seat and was looking at me questioningly, smilingly, cheerfully, Spanishly.

I said it again. "Players Theatre?" I said it less hopefully this time.

He smiled just as charmingly. "*Qué?*"

I had never been in Miami before, I didn't know where the hell the Players put on their plays. Even if I had known, I didn't see how I could explain it to him, and I was really in no condition to even make a good effort.

I got out of the cab and tried the next one in line. It was also Spanish. I looked down the long line and every one of them was Spanish. I looked around for a dispatcher. I had no great hopes that he wouldn't also be Spanish, but we'll never know because he simply didn't exist.

What could I do? I managed to walk back into the terminal and found a newsstand and bought a paper. There was an ad for the Players' current production, and it gave the name of the theater: the Coconut Grove. I hoped that would be enough.

It was. I showed the paper to the cabby, pointing at the ad, and he looked at it and smiled happily and nodded. I didn't have much hope of actually getting there but, as I said, I was in no condition to argue. So we hopped in and roared off, and finally did make it there just in time to catch the show.

The less said about which the better. Never mind. I hate drama critics, I'm not about to become one. But the thought of what John Simon would have said about this production kept me alternately giggling and shuddering through the second act. At least it kept me awake.

I had hoped—not seriously, but on the outer fringes of my mind—that perhaps she might be in this play. It was possible, wasn't it? I might have sat down in my seat and watched the curtain rise and seen her walk right out of the Polaroid photos and onto the stage.

But she didn't. Which didn't bother me. What I had really hoped for was to find someone that I knew, someone I could talk to, ask questions of. And I found him. The second lead—the "comic" lead in this production—was a guy named Morris Delmingo with whom I had done time in Indiana.

After the show I went backstage and found him.

"Hey, *paisano!*" he shouted, and hugged me. He's a big man, a fat man, which is maybe why the director saw his character as comic. That's the way directors think. "What are you doing here in Miami?"

"Better than Indiana, I guess." I tried to hug him back but couldn't get my arms around him.

"In Spiritu Domini," he whispered, and made the sign. "Come out for some pizza?"

"Why not?" I sat down and watched him take off his makeup, and we made small talk. Which made it come out nice and casual when I said, "Hey, by the way," and pulled the girl's picture out of my pocket and showed it to him. "Know her?"

His fingers were greasy with cold cream so he didn't take it. But he leaned over and looked at it and said, "Uh-uh."

"Hell. I thought she worked here."

"Nope."

"We're thinking of beginning to cast my new play, and I half remember her from somewhere, and I thought . . ." I shrugged.

"What's her name?"

"I don't know."

He looked at me like he thought I was a little weird. "Sure," he said.

"Look, what I mean—"

He lifted his eyebrows like other people lift their hands. "Don't *hok* me a *chainik, bubeleh*, I couldn't care less. You got maybe a little something for me in your new play?"

"What can I tell you? There's really nothing right for you in it. But you know I'll keep you in mind. Speaking of right for you, what's with this character you're playing? Since when is he for laughs?"

He rolled his eyes and pantomimed falling off the chair onto his back and dying. "Did you ever see such a *bobbe-*

myself? I wish you'd been at rehearsal. I gave the best performance of my life—offstage. Begging our director to just for one moment think about the *concept*. I pleaded, I cried, I flagellated myself—"

"You always did enjoy that," I said. "You know this guy?" I showed him the Polaroid of the guy.

"Sure," he said. "Billy Noel. Anyway, I literally went down on my knees for the son of a bitch—not what you're thinking, but I would have done that, too. But to no avail—"

"Who's Billy Noel?"

"He's playing one of the gamblers in *Three Men*, that's our next production. So anyhow, the son of a bitch tells me that according to Stanislavsky, for God's sake, can you believe it, according to . . ."

He came in while we were having pizza. I had already written down his name and address, intending to go see him first thing in the morning, and was sitting with a half dozen of the gang around a big round table having pizza when he walked in. "There he is," Morris said.

"Who?"

"Billy." I looked around, and Morris was already calling him over. "Hey, Billy, come over here, buddy of mine wants to cast you in his big new New York hit show."

I stood up and shook hands. "Not exactly," I said quickly. I didn't want to build up false hopes; I knew how quickly they built and how high, and how nasty the fall was. "I want to talk to you if you have a minute." I gestured to another table, a smaller one for two, on the other side of the restaurant, and he followed me over.

"I didn't get your name," he said, sitting down.

"Henry Grace," I said.

He looked at me blankly. Pleasantly, but blankly. He

was good-looking, dark curly hair, slender like me, maybe an inch shorter. He was looking at me with the expression of an actor who has been introduced to someone who maybe has a job for him but who has denied it, so maybe there's something but what the hell. Nothing more than that.

"Henry Grace," I repeated.

He nodded.

"You don't know me?" I asked.

He shrugged. "Sorry, I don't remember. Where did we meet?"

"We haven't met," I said. "I'm a friend of Turner's."

"Turner?" For a moment he was puzzled, then recognition came. "Oh, sure," he said. And smiled. Nothing special, just a nice, pleasant actor's smile.

I took one of the Polaroid snaps out of my pocket and handed it across the table to him.

He looked at it, smiled and nodded, then frowned. "When Morris said you wanted to cast me—"

"No," I said. "I don't do sex shows."

"Okay, then. 'Cause neither do I."

"You did that." I gestured to the photo.

"That was pleasure, not business," he said, and the frown deepened. "How'd you get this, anyhow?"

I sighed. A detective's life is not as easy as it sounds. "I was hoping you'd say you had sent it to me," I told him.

He shook his head.

"Someone sent it to me anonymously," I told him.

"Why?"

"Turner's wife is dead."

"So?"

"I thought maybe there was some connection."

"What?"

"I don't know what. I was hoping you could tell me."

He shook his head. "I don't like people mailing these pictures around, you know? It was personal, you know what I mean?"

"Who has any of them? If you didn't mail them, who could have?"

"Just Cissy and Turner."

"Cissy is the girl?"

He nodded. "Cissy Massenick."

"Where's she live?"

"Somewhere in town, on the beach, I think."

"You don't know?"

He shook his head. "I don't see her that often. I've got it written down at home if you need it."

"She's Turner's friend, then?"

He nodded.

"Tell me about them."

"Why should I?"

I shrugged. I didn't want to tell him I was a private undercover dick. Word like that would travel through the acting fraternity like a diuretic. I'd never be taken seriously as a playwright again. So I shrugged, and he looked at me, and I did a very subtle thing with my eyes and just a twitch of the lips and I think maybe he got the impression that I was a bit more than a friend of Turner's. Anyway, he began to talk.

"I don't know them that well," he said. "It was really just this one time. A few months ago. I was over at the Castaways, just having a few drinks, and Cissy was there with this guy. Turner. So you know, we talked a little and I sat down with them, and everything got cool. After a few hours Cissy asked if I wanted to go back with them."

"She asked you?"

"Well, I guess maybe she sort of asked both of us. I don't remember exactly. We were all kind of stoned by then. Anyway, that's what we **did**. We went back to her place and fooled around, and she had this Polaroid and we took some snaps. Just good, clean fun, you know what I mean? Nothing weird."

"And you each kept some of the snapshots?"

"Yeah. As a souvenir, you know? No big deal. Only they shouldn't go mailing them around the country."

"How friendly were Turner and Cissy?"

He shrugged. He looked through the pile of snapshots, pulled one out, and slid it across the table. It was of Turner and Cissy. "That's pretty friendly, I'd say."

"That's not what I mean. Would they be thinking of anything serious? Getting married, anything like that?"

He looked through the pictures again, selected another one, and showed it to me. It was of him and Cissy. "Does a guy take shots of his wife-to-be and another guy like that?" Then he thought about it. "I don't know." He smiled at me. "It's a big world out there. All kinds of guys. I just don't know."

CHAPTER 7

Oh, God.

I woke up with the inside of my mouth tasting like the outside of a tennis ball, and the inside of my head feeling like Borg was in there volleying my teeth across the net.

It was that cognac after dinner on the airplane. I can't drink cognac. It couldn't have been the beer. God wouldn't be cruel enough to punish people for drinking beer, but cognac drinkers deserve what they get.

Thank God for my masochistic upbringing, which enabled me to sit up. At first I didn't know where I was. At first I didn't care. Slowly it came back to me. I was at Morris' on his couch. Why was I awake?

It was all coming back now. One thing I brag about is an inner chronometer/alarm that never fails. I had told myself last night to wake up at eight this morning, and now here I was at eight in the morning on Morris' couch sitting up and wide awake, wondering if I should vomit or just die.

After another ten minutes, during which it might have gone either way and I wouldn't really have cared, I decided to try a cup of coffee instead. Slowly I returned to the land of the living, more or less.

I had set my system for eight o'clock because I had to get over to Billy Noel's place and pick up Cissy's address before he left for rehearsal. He had said he had an eleven o'clock call this morning.

So I had some more coffee and left about nine, without waking Morris. I washed and dressed and tiptoed to the front door and opened it—

And wow, there it all was! I mean, just like in the television ads. Back in New York at nine o'clock this morning, if it was anything like yesterday, the sun was only a dim rumor, the sky was thick and grumpy and dark gray, and the air was full of wind and water and irritating specks of dirt that caught under your eyelids and in your throat. But here—now I knew why people come to Miami to live. The sky was blue, brilliant blue, and the few clouds were white and a joy to behold. The sun was bright and the air sparkled and my hangover slunk away in shame.

I followed Morris' instructions, walking down the street and through Coconut Grove. In New York I would have caught a bus. In Miami you can't catch a bus from anywhere to anywhere, but it was such a pleasure to walk I didn't care. I thought maybe someday I'd retire down here.

I found Noel's place and knocked on the door. It was a wooden cottage surrounded by foliage, falling apart but with a certain charm. It was about nine-thirty in the morning.

I knocked again.

There was no answer.

I was hit with a spasm of unease. I should have come home with him last night—but I couldn't have done that. I didn't exactly pass out, but we were drinking a lot of beer with some lousy pizza, and I sort of don't exactly remember what happened at the end. To be honest, I don't quite remember getting back to Morris' pad. I don't remember leaving Billy.

But we'd made a date for this morning. So where the hell was he?

I began to remind myself that what I was investigating was a murder. Murder is contagious. What if—

The door opened. A short, thin man with a long, thick beard stood there.

"Billy home?" I asked.

He shook his head.

"I was supposed to meet him this morning," I said. "I was supposed to see him before he left for rehearsal—"

"Hell, that's Billy for you. Come on in," he said. "I'm Jim Cartin, I don't guess he mentioned me."

"Not exactly."

"I share this place. Come on in, make yourself to home. Billy ought to be in any minute."

"He had an eleven o'clock call for rehearsal—"

"Hell, then he'll be in any minute. He didn't come home last night."

I must have looked suddenly worried, because he laughed. "Hell, man, that's Billy all over. You never know when that son of a bitch is gonna sleep home. Who was he with last night?"

"Nobody in particular."

"It don't have to be nobody in particular. That acting crowd, right? Boy, I just wish he'd take me along once in a while, that's all I wish. Want some coffee?"

"Okay."

"I just got some brewed. I'll pour it out while you go on in there and wash up your hands. Go on, now." He pointed the way to the bathroom in the rear of the cottage. Somewhat reluctantly, I went along. My hands didn't need washing.

He stood in the entrance to the kitchen, waiting for me to go in. You could tell he was holding something in. I opened the door to the bathroom and went in.

And I saw what he was going on about. You couldn't

help but see it. See them. Pictures. All over the wall. Nicely framed, nicely arranged. Polaroid shots, one and all. Some in color. All of Billy Noel and various friends. Male and female. I looked at each of them. They were really interesting, if you like that sort of thing. I think they must have been interesting even if you didn't. I looked at each of them, starting over the sink and moving to the wall over the commode, and I found it. One of the pictures was of him and Turner and Cissy. Not one of the ones that had been sent to me, but obviously from that group, taken at the same time.

I washed my hands and went back to the kitchen. Jim was standing over two cups of coffee, waiting for me, grinning. "How about that, hey?" he asked. "Is that something? So now you know where Billy is."

"Does he always bring back a picture?"

"Hell no! If he *always* brought back a picture we could wallpaper the house. Twice a year! Boy, he's some guy, Billy. I just wish he'd take me along once in a while."

We had the coffee and it was getting on for ten o'clock. Jim said Billy'd be sure to stop in to change before rehearsal, but he had to get to work and did I want to wait? I said yes, if he didn't mind. He didn't mind.

"Ain't nothing to steal," he said. "Except them pictures. And I guess we'll always have a supply of them. You know, you wanta hear something funny?"

I said sure.

"Every once in a while he'll bring home some broad he just met and, well, sooner or later she's gonna go in the can, right? You oughta see their faces when they come out." He laughed at the memory. "Sometimes they'll come out like there was nothing in there, like they didn't notice nothing, you know what I mean? Most of the time, though," he confided, "it turns them on, you know? Like you can tell, when they come out."

He shook his head ruefully. "I brought a girl back here once," he said. "We had some beer and then she went in the can, and I was just waiting here for her, you know? Son of a bitch, if she didn't come out and walk right out of here! Didn't say a goddamn word, just came out and walked right past me without even a look or a good-bye or anything, just walked on out of here and I never saw *her* again." He shook his head. "Goddamn. I just wish Billy'd take me along once in a while, meet some of *his* friends."

After he left I settled down to wait. Then I got up and wandered around a bit. I have to admit I wandered back into the bathroom. The pictures really were kind of interesting. I found that I recognized a couple of the girls.

Then I wandered back into the living room and sat down again. It got to be after ten o'clock. I decided to wander on into his bedroom. After all, I was investigating a murder, wasn't I?

There was a one-drawer desk piled high with scripts and *New York* magazines and correspondence. I looked through the correspondence, but there was nothing to or from Turner. I found an address book and looked through it. Cissy was listed there, and I copied down her address.

That was what I had come for, and I suppose I could have left at this point. But I was wondering why he hadn't come home yet. He still had time, of course, the rehearsal call wasn't until eleven, and the theater was less than fifteen minutes from here. I figured he'd be home to change before eleven at the latest, and it was after ten now, so what the hell, I might as well wait. I decided I wouldn't get worried until eleven o'clock.

At five after eleven I decided not to get worried at all. There was no big need to change before rehearsal. So he'd overslept and gone straight off to rehearsal in yesterday's clothes. He probably hadn't remembered that we had arranged to meet this morning, and even if he had he wouldn't have thought it was important enough to worry about. Actors as a rule are not the most considerate people in the world.

I could have called the theater just to be sure he was safely at rehearsal, but I felt too self-conscious to do that. Playing private eye is okay, but you have to keep it within bounds, right? Mustn't let the imagination run wild. Mustn't see murders peeping out of every dark corner. Dark corners are scary enough without that. After all, I had Cissy's address. That was what I had come here for.

I decided to wait just five minutes more. Till ten past eleven.

At nine minutes past, the policeman came.

Jim had left the front door open when he left, but the screen door was closed and that was what the cop knocked on. When I came to the door he asked if I was Billy Noel. I said no.

He nodded as if that was the answer he'd been expecting. "Does Mr. Noel live here?"

I said yes. "Is something wrong?" I asked.

"Are you a relative of Mr. Noel's?"

"No. A friend. I'm waiting for him to come home."

"Would you know the name of any relative of his in Miami?"

"No, I don't think he has any. He's from New York. Is something wrong?"

"Could you describe Mr. Noel, please?"

"About six foot," I said, "maybe an inch or two over

that. About my height. Slender, almost thin. Dark, curly hair. Blue eyes. Something *is* wrong. What is it?"

"You wouldn't happen to know what Mr. Noel was wearing last night?"

"Jeans, and a red striped shirt. What's this all about?"

He nodded. "A body that fits your description was found sometime after three o'clock this morning. A wallet was just found a couple of blocks away, with no money but Mr. Noel's driver's license. We need somebody to identify the body."

My feet were cold and my knees were shaking, but he didn't seem to notice. "What happened to him?"

"What is your name, sir?"

I told him.

"Address?"

I told him.

"Nature of your relationship to Mr. Noel?"

I didn't know what to say. My knees were still shaking and my brain was all shaken. "I'm a playwright," I said. "He's an actor."

That seemed all right. He had been writing my answers down. Now he put his notebook away. I didn't want to ask him again, but I had to. I didn't want to know what had happened, but I had to. Maybe it was just an accident. Maybe a heart attack. Oh, God, please let him have had a heart attack. And somebody saw him lying there in the street and figured he might just as well lift his wallet. I didn't want to know. . . .

"What happened to him?" I asked.

The cop shrugged. "Knife in the guts," he said.

Well, it was Metropolitan Dade County's two hundred and forty-seventh homicide of the year, and nobody seemed very excited about it. Metropolitan Dade County is what they call Miami, and two hundred and forty-seven homicides is one hell of a lot. It's up nearly 50 percent from last year, which was up nearly 50 percent from the year before.

It's a funny thing. You take any city, you're going to have a certain number of murders. If the number is pretty constant every year and then suddenly one year starts to go up, people get excited. They talk about the breakdown of law and order, and they raise the taxes and hire more cops, and in general they get very upset about it. But if a few years go by and the homicide rate keeps on climbing, a funny thing happens. You'd think people would get more and more upset about it. But they don't. They stop getting upset. They start saying things like, "Well, hell, that's just human nature," and they begin to quote statistics that show that most of the homicides take place in the ghetto and the victims are black, and what with one thing and another they calm themselves down.

That's the state Metropolitan Dade County is in today. Every day the *Herald* publishes a very short article listing the day's murder victims, and nobody gets very excited about them.

It begins to sound like a contest. "Come on, everybody, let's all get together now and see if we can beat last year's record!" They'll do it, too.

Anyway, the body was found shortly after 3 A.M., the victim of a mugging. Without question. Knifed body found in the street, wallet found empty a few blocks away.

It doesn't sound like much. Routine. But all of a sudden this private-eye game didn't seem like so much fun.

I left the police station and found a coin telephone in a drugstore. I dropped a dime in the slot. Nothing happened. No dial tone. It was going to be one of those days.

I banged the phone. Nothing. I jiggled the return handle and my dime came back. I dropped it in again. Again no dial tone.

There was another phone next to it. I got my dime back and moved to it. Same story. Finally, when all else fails, read the instructions. Goddamn. It costs twenty-five cents to make a phone call in Miami. Twenty-five cents, can you believe it?

So I dropped in a quarter and dialed Cissy's number. It rang three times, then a voice said, "Hello. This is Cissy Massenick—"

"Hello," I started, "my name is—"

"—and I'm not home right now. But I'd sure like to talk to you! If you'll leave your name and phone number when you hear the beep I'll call you right back. Honest! 'Bye now." . . . Beep! . . .

I had lunch at the counter and then called again and got the same recording. It occurred to me that at twenty-five cents a throw this might turn out to be an expensive call. And I didn't like the idea of just going there and waiting on her front step.

I decided to try Morris' pad. Maybe he'd be home this afternoon and I could wait there and keep calling till I got Cissy. So I started on over there, but on the way I passed Billy Noel's corner. Without thinking much about it I turned up the street. Maybe Jim would be home.

I knocked on the door, but nobody answered. As I was turning away I tried the door. Not really expecting anything, you know what I mean? But it opened.

I stood there for a moment.

I stuck my head in and called, "Jim?"

I didn't like it.

To tell the truth, I was scared.

Maybe I had left the door unlocked when I left. I tried

to think back. But I'd been so upset when the cop told me what had happened that I couldn't remember. Maybe I *had* left it unlocked.

Maybe Jim was in the bathroom, where he wouldn't have heard me calling him. I bet he spends a lot of time in that bathroom.

I opened the door and took a step in. I called, "Hey, Jim!"

No answer.

Empty houses are spooky. Especially if someone's just been killed. Mugged. *Maybe* mugged. How did I know? Maybe it was Turner that stuck that knife in his guts. That's what I was thinking, standing there in the doorway of that empty house.

Maybe Turner was in that empty house.

But that was stupid. I stepped in. I called again, "Hey there, Jim?"

I wasn't afraid, I told myself.

I would look through the house. I left the front door open. Somehow that helped, as if I could turn around and run through it if I had to.

I walked through the living room, calling Jim. I checked the bathroom. Jim wasn't there. I stepped back out into the—

I stopped. I had seen something in that bathroom, and I didn't want to see it. I wasn't sure if I *had* seen it. I didn't want to look again.

I had to.

I turned around and stepped back into the bathroom. And I saw it. Or rather, I *didn't* see it. I didn't see the picture of Billy Noel and Cissy Massenick and Turner. There was just a blank space on the wall where it had been.

At first I wasn't sure. Maybe I didn't remember the layout properly. There was no definite order to the pictures. I looked at all of them quickly. Turner's picture wasn't there. I looked again. Yes, if you looked closely you could see the small hole where the hook had been.

Someone had taken it.

Someone had been in here.

Someone might still be here.

Someone? Turner.

Who else? Who else would take that picture?

Oh, Christ, and I was alone in here.

I had goose pimples on my back. And on my legs. My legs were suddenly very cold. I was the only person in Miami with cold legs.

I was the only person in that house. I *hoped* I was the only person in that house. I wished I knew. I wished I had a gun. I hate guns. I wouldn't know how to shoot one. But I wished I had one.

I straightened up and looked around the bathroom. It was empty, there's no place where anyone can hide in a bathroom—

Oh no. Oh, my God.

The curtain. The bathtub curtain was drawn closed. I stood there and stared at it, and all I could think of was *Psycho*.

I tried to remember if it had been closed when I was in there earlier this morning. I just couldn't remember. I stood there and stared at it. Oh, Christ, I was scared. I was sure there was somebody behind that curtain, Turner was behind that curtain—

I saw Sarah's body crumpled on the floor and I saw Billy Noel's body cold in the morgue with a gaping hole slashed out of his belly and Turner was waiting there behind the curtain, waiting for me to turn around—

I was afraid to turn and run, I was afraid to stand there

and wait, I was afraid to do anything, but I had to do something.

I held my breath, I lifted my hand, suddenly, suddenly I grabbed the curtain and yanked it open—

There was no one there.

For a second I thought I would faint.

I stepped out of the bathroom. I shouted, "Jim!" I made a lot of noise. If anyone—if Turner—was still in that house he'd hear me. I wanted to give him plenty of time to sneak away.

I came out of the bathroom and stood there awhile, then turned right into the kitchen. It was empty. There was nowhere to hide in the kitchen. But I was so scared I was afraid to open the refrigerator, I was sure there'd be a body in there. Cissy's body. Too many late movies on television.

I opened the drawers, looked through them, and found a knife. A big, old-fashioned knife. I don't know what I thought I needed it for, if there was a body in the refrigerator it'd be a dead body, not somebody waiting there to jump out at me. But I took the knife. I stood in front of the refrigerator. I opened the door—

"Boo!"

Christ! I screamed. I jumped. I whirled around and slashed out with the knife.

"Hey!" he screamed back at me, falling away as fast as he could. "Hey, man, what the hell you doing?"

It was Jim.

I stood there staring at him. I dropped the knife. My heart was thumping. I was shaking. "Don't *do* things like that," I said.

"Hey, I was only fooling," he said. "I didn't know you were the nervous type."

I sat down in the kitchen chair and he put on some

coffee and told me he'd come home and found the door open, so he came sneaking in, he thought it was some kid breaking in to steal the stereo or the pictures. And when he saw me he thought it'd be fun to sneak up on me and shout "Boo."

He was right. It was a lot of fun.

He was lucky I hadn't slashed his goddamn nose off when I whirled around. I wish I had. Instead, I told him about Billy.

I didn't tell him about the missing picture. While I was telling him about Billy I was thinking about that. If I told him we'd have to tell the police, and I didn't want to get involved with them here. It was all part of what had happened to Sarah, and I wanted to get back to Karen Douglass and let her handle it from there.

But Cissy?

I called, and got the same recording. I thought, at least she's not home, she's out somewhere safe. And then I thought, maybe she's not answering the phone because she's lying in an alley with her throat cut. Never mind they don't have alleys in Miami. She could be lying on her own bedroom floor with her throat cut while that phone rings and the recorded voice of a dead woman answers it cheerfully and automatically forever and ever. . . .

Or she could be out somewhere shopping for a new bathing suit to wear on this beautiful afternoon in Miami, and Turner could be waiting there outside her apartment, waiting for her to come home. Waiting to kill her.

Why would he want to kill her?

Answer: Why did he want to kill Billy Noel? Why did somebody send me those pictures?

Who sent the pictures?

Answer: Cissy. No one else had them. It wasn't Billy, and it sure as hell wasn't Turner.

Must find Cissy. Must get to her before Turner does. Must find out why she sent the pictures. What have they to do with Sarah's murder? Must find Cissy before he kills her.

She lived in Coral Gables, a much fancier neighborhood. I couldn't walk there. And like I said, the buses in Miami never go from anywhere you are to anywhere you want to go. I had to take a cab. The cab rates down here are ruinous. Much worse than New York. Tourist town. I hoped Cissy would have a car to give me a lift back out to the airport.

The cab driver at least spoke English, which was something.

I was lucky he did, because we had trouble finding her pied-à-terre. The address was 9360 La Hacienda—that's the kind of street name they have in Coral Gables—and we found 9350, but then the next house was 9380. We drove back and forth a couple times and then he said, "It's probably a garage. What used to be a garage. In back of the house. They don't have enough money, you know, they have to rent out their garages. They don't make enough money importing coke."

"Everybody down here pushes coke?"

"How else you gonna make enough money to buy one of them suckers?" He gestured at the homes on La Hacienda. "You know what they cost? Any one of 'em? Nobody knows what they cost, 'cause you find out what one of them costs and by the time you tell your wife the price's gone up another twenny thousand. Cocaine cowboys, nobody else can buy one of them. Cocaine cowboys and doctors, nobody else."

I paid him without telling him what I thought of the cab rates in Miami. I walked up the driveway of 9350, and he was right. When I reached the spot where the driveway curved to pass in front of the house, I could see where it used to continue to what was now a converted garage out behind. I walked on back there, across the grass. I knocked on the door. There was no answer.

I was scared. But only nervous scared, not terrified like I was back in Billy's cottage. It's something psychological. Something about being *inside* an empty house there and being *outside* one here. There was the feeling there of being trapped, the feeling here that I could always turn and run like hell.

I looked back at the house. It was quiet. I walked around the garage. The shades were drawn, but they didn't quite come all the way down and I could peek in. I didn't see a body lying anywhere, I didn't see any blood. I came back around to the front of the garage. The grounds were empty, and I couldn't imagine Turner hiding behind a tree.

I sat down on the little stoop at the front door. I leaned back against the doorjamb and closed my eyes in the warm sunshine and wondered what I should do. Maybe she was out shopping, maybe she'd be back in an hour. Maybe not.

I decided what I ought to do first was go up to the house behind which this garage sat and ask if they knew where she might be. I yawned and stretched and opened my eyes, and there was a woman standing there.

I hadn't heard her walk across the grass. I'm a New York boy, I'm not used to people walking on grass. My first thought was, it could have been Turner and he could have killed me. Some private eye.

"Can I help you?" she asked.

She was a little old lady, gray hair piled up high on her head. She looked like Helen Hayes. She held her hands together in front of her belly and she leaned forward a little. Probably just a bit hard of hearing.

"I'm just waiting for Cissy," I said.

"You don't have to shout, you know. I may be getting on in years but I can still hear perfectly well."

I hadn't shouted, but I apologized anyway. "Do you know if she'll be back soon?"

"What?"

I said it again, a bit louder.

She shook her head.

"Do you know where she is?" I asked.

"I'm afraid I don't."

"I guess I'll wait, then, if you don't mind."

She looked as if she wanted to say something. She obviously didn't like the idea of my waiting there. She couldn't figure out quite what to say, and she walked back to the house. She stood by the back door, looking over her shoulder at me. I smiled at her. It didn't seem to reassure her. I leaned back and closed my eyes.

It wasn't very restful, though. I had this continual feeling that she was staring at me. I fought a losing battle to keep my eyes closed against the pressure of her stare. I lost.

I opened my eyes, and she was standing right there in front of me again. I wished she wouldn't keep on doing that.

"Are you just going to wait there?" she asked.

"I thought I would."

"But you can't wait there forever."

"Just until she comes back."

She was struggling for the right words. "But it will be a long time," she said.

"Do you know how long?"

She shook her head.

"Then I guess I'll just have to wait."
"But where will you sleep?"
"Sleep?"
"It may be weeks," she said. She was certainly troubled.
"You don't know where she is?" I asked gently.
She shook her head.
"Has she gone away?" I asked.
She smiled, relieved. "Yes," she said. That was the right word. "Cissy's gone away."
"For good?"
"Oh no. A vacation, you know."
"Out of town?"
"Oh yes. Somewhere up north."
Oh, Christ. And I was going to sit here waiting for her. "And you don't know where she is or when she'll be back?"
She looked at me suspiciously. "Is it a job?"
"What?"
"Are you looking for her for a job? She's an actress, you know. Well, she *wants* to be an actress but she doesn't get many jobs. She was on television once. She said if her agent called about a job . . . I wasn't expecting anyone to actually come right here about a job, I thought they'd call. On the phone, you know."
"I'm a writer," I said. "I do have a job for her, if I can find her. I did call, but all I got was her recording."
"Oh, you should have called us. She said she gave our number to her agent."
"What would you have done if I had called?"
"What?"
"If I had called. With a job for her. You said you don't know where she is."
"Oh, I *don't* know. But she left her address. Where she

is. She left it in her typewriter, she said. If her agent called, I was to just go in and read it to him."

I sighed. She looked at me quizzically. I smiled. "Could we do that, then? Could we go in and look at the address she left in her typewriter?"

She didn't seem keen on doing that. I don't know, I guess I must look like a suspicious character. But I smiled, and kept on smiling until she unwrapped one of her hands from the other and reached down into a pocket and brought out a ring of keys and opened the door to the converted garage, and I followed her in.

I glanced around and saw a desk with a typewriter on it. I walked quickly over to it. Helen Hayes stood by the door. She obviously didn't think it proper to enter another person's house, even with permission. She wouldn't have liked anyone entering her own house in her absence, for any reason whatsoever.

There was a paper in the typewriter. It said simply: "George's Rentals, P.O. Box 389, Diana's Trail, N.Y. 14835."

That was in upstate New York, somewhere in the Finger Lakes region.

"Is she camping out?" I asked. "Is that what she liked?"

Helen smiled. "I don't know."

I sat down at the typewriter. "Has anyone else been here?" I asked. "Anybody else asking for Cissy?"

She shook her head.

"No one offering her a job?" I asked. "You haven't shown anyone else this note?"

"No," she said.

I nodded. "I'll just retype this note and take a copy, all right?"

She nodded.

I took out the paper from the typewriter, inserted a clean sheet. I typed: *Screw you, Turner. The Phantom strikes again.*

I was feeling pretty good.

I put the paper with her address on it in my pocket and walked to the door. Miss Hayes waited as I preceded her out, to be sure I didn't steal a vase, I suppose, and then she carefully followed me out and relocked the door. She rattled the knob hard to make sure it was locked.

I was feeling damned good. I knew where she was and Turner didn't, and now there was no way he could find out. He had caught Billy Noel, but Cissy was safe somewhere up there at George's Rentals.

I smiled and said good-bye and left Miss Hayes standing there on the grass watching me go.

If I had known what was happening as I walked down La Hacienda Avenue looking for a cab to take me to the airport, I wouldn't have felt so pretty damned good.

If I had known then what I didn't find out until it was too late, in fact, I would have been pretty damned worried.

I would have been terrified.

And a nightmare might have been avoided.

But I didn't know. I didn't know that as I was whistling my way down to South Dixie Highway and finding a pay phone and calling a cab, Miss Helen Hayes was going back into her house.

"Where you been?" her husband asked.

"Just out back. I didn't go anywhere."

"Wish you'd tell me when you go out."

"Just out back."

"Even out back. I worry, you know. Don't want you wandering off."

"I wouldn't wander off. I just went out back."

"Well, okay then."

And as I was waiting for the cab to come to take me to the plane to take me back to New York, her husband asked, "Why'd you go out back, anyway?"

"There was a young man there."

"What?"

"A young man. Looking for Cissy."

"Another job?"

"That's what he said, yes."

"You tell him where she is?"

"I don't *know* where she is."

"But you showed him the note she left?"

"I let him in the garage. He looked at the note. I didn't go in myself. Not all the way in. I don't think that's right."

"But you showed him the note?"

"He *looked* at the note. He looked himself. *I* didn't look."

"Well, that's all right then. Two jobs for Cissy, that's pretty good. Maybe she'll be a star yet."

"No."

"Maybe she will. Pretty as a picture, that girl."

"I mean no, not two jobs. He only had one job for her."

"Right, one job. And that fellow yesterday, that makes *two* jobs."

"Yesterday?"

"You remember, that young man yesterday? Came looking for Cissy? I took him out to the garage, gave him her address. You remember?"

"Oh, *that* young man," Helen Hayes said. "I forgot."

CHAPTER 8

I got into Idlewild at 7:15 P.M. Yes, I know, its name is Kennedy. Everybody calls it Kennedy. I still call it Idlewild. It's not a political thing. It's onomatopoeic. Idlewild *sounds* like an airport.

So anyhow, I got in at seven-fifteen. I figured the easiest thing to do was just take the train from Jamaica out to Patchogue and check in with the *pizzella* that night, instead of calling her in the morning and probably having to go all the way out from the city.

I called the police station from the train station in Patchogue. She wasn't there. I hadn't thought she would be. It was about ten o'clock by then. I asked for her home number. They wouldn't give it to me. They said they'd give her a message. I said for them to tell her it was me and I was waiting at the train station and that it was definitely murder most foul.

I got the call-back in ten minutes. It was from the butler. Swear to God, the *butler*. He said that Miss Karen was on her way to pick me up.

It was cold at the station. It seemed colder inside, so I walked up and down on the platform. In Miami it was seventy-eight degrees, and there would be no clouds hiding the moon. A gust of wind came rushing in over the salt marshes and almost knocked me down. I could feel a little tickle beginning in my sinus.

The Jag came cutting around the corner and I hurried

down to meet it. As the inside light came on I saw she was in a long gown with a fur jacket slung over her shoulders. I slid in beside her and slammed the door. It was warm and comfy. I guess if you can afford fur jackets and a Jag it doesn't matter where you live.

"Did I interrupt something?" I asked, gesturing at her dress.

"A party. Nothing important, one of Daddy's. We'll go back to the house and talk there. Is that all right? We could go to the station if you prefer."

"Probably the scotch will be better at Daddy's," I said.

She gave me a cool glance out of the corner of her eyes, and we whizzed off down the Sunrise Highway.

We didn't talk on the way. I wanted my tale to have the proper setting and to come out as a dramatic whole rather than piece by piece, and I suppose she felt the same way. So we sat quietly and roared off toward the Hamptons.

She drove well. We pulled into a circular driveway, coasted to a stop, and she clicked off the ignition. The house was full of lights and noise. I resisted the impulse to make a witty remark about Versailles or Fontainebleau being open late this evening. Somehow I had the impression she wouldn't think it was funny.

It looked like a great party. The women were in sort of formal things, like she was. The men were wearing tuxes. There were a few slobs there in dark suits. I was wearing jeans, but I didn't feel too bad because they were genuine Levi's. On the other hand, my shirt was vintage Penney's and my jacket was Goodwill. At times like this I wish I smoked. You look more cool with a cigarette dangling from your lips. I don't know how I looked, but I sure didn't *feel* cool moving through the crowd.

The *pizzella* moved well, like she belonged. Of course,

she *did* belong, but you could see she'd move like that anywhere, in the police station, at college, anywhere. She *was* cool. She looked like Kate Hepburn. Some cop.

She guided me through the party and into an empty room. Lined with books. A bay window and a window-seat. Dark paneling. Real wood, you could tell by the smell, not plastic-coated plywood. A library, the real thing. She guided me in and closed the door behind me, disappearing back into the party. When the door closed, the sound of the party disappeared. I mean, it cut off like *that*. Just like in the movies. I didn't know they made insulation that good.

I never mind waiting in a room like that. I wandered around and checked the books. Shakespeare and Shaw and O'Casey, of course. O'Neill and Chekhov. And John Arden and Arnold Wesker and Bernard Kops and Sam Shepard. No Neil Simon. I could grow to love a girl like that.

She came back in with a glass of beer and another young lady. "This is Charlotte Steward," she said. "She's Daddy's secretary. She's agreed to give up the party for a bit to take down your statement, if that's all right? And this"—she indicated the beer—"is Beck's Dark. If you'd really rather have scotch, I can get you some."

I told her that both Charlotte and Beck's would be fine. We sat down and got comfortable. The door opened again and Turner came in.

Talk about being flabbergasted. I was flummoxed.

He was wearing a tux and carrying a drink. He had a cigarette dangling from his lip. He looked cool, he looked like he belonged, he looked like a goddamn *guest* at this party!

He came in and sat down with us. He crossed his feet and leaned back and sipped his drink.

Karen smiled. "I was as surprised as you obviously are," she said to me, "to find that Turner was a guest of Daddy's tonight."

"Moving up in the world, Turner," I said. "Crashing society."

He shrugged expansively. "*C'est la guerre*," he said. "The *economic* war, you know. One wins a battle, then a campaign, and suddenly one finds oneself moving with the traditional victors."

"*Does* one?"

He smiled.

"We've been having an interesting conversation," Karen said, "Turner and I. I asked him to sit in on your statement. I'd like his reaction. If you don't mind?"

"No," I said, looking right at him. "I don't mind. I'd like to see his reaction, too."

"Good. Then let's begin."

"Right. I flew down to—"

"First give your full name and address, so Charlotte can get it down in the record. Then go ahead and tell us everything."

So I began to tell them everything. At first I spoke slowly, but Charlotte had no problem keeping up with me and soon I was talking normally.

I started off by saying that I had flown down to Miami yesterday afternoon. I kept my eyes on Turner as I said that, wanting to see the effect. The son of a bitch is tough, I have to give him that. He didn't blanch. His only reaction was a minuscule motion of the eyes, dropping them momentarily toward the tip of his cigarette, then lifting them again and meeting my stare eyeball to eyeball. I give him that, he's a tough son of a bitch. Nobody else in that room caught the flicker of his eye.

I told them that I found Billy Noel.

"Who is that?" the *pizzella* interrupted.

"The guy in the Polaroids," I told her. I repeated what Billy had told me. Then I told them that Billy was dead.

Silence in the room.

"How?" she asked.

"Knifed," I said. I told them how I had met him last night and had made an appointment this morning that he hadn't shown up for. "Knifed," I repeated. "Killed the same way Sarah was killed."

Silence. Just the sound of the secretary's pen writing on her pad for a few seconds after my last words, then total silence.

"Killed by the same person that killed Sarah," I said.

Silence.

"It might have been a random mugging," the *pizzella* said.

So I told her about the pictures in Billy's bathroom. I told her about the missing picture. I told *her* about it, but I kept my eyes on Turner. Not one motion out of him, not a grimace. Not the blink of an eye.

I told them I went to Cissy's house—

"Who is Cissy?"

"The girl in the Polaroids," I said. "Billy gave me her address. I wanted to find her before Turner killed her, too—"

"Goddamn it, hold on!" Turner interrupted. "I didn't kill anyone!"

I smiled. I'd been waiting for him to crack.

But that was all he said. He turned and looked at Karen, and she looked from one of us to the other. Then she asked Turner, "Would you like to say something at this point?"

He nodded.

He hesitated.

"I don't like saying this," he finally said. "But there are some things that must be said. My wife is dead. I assumed she'd been killed by a burglar. Then you showed me some pictures and asked me if I recognized them. I didn't—"

"You can drop that game," I told him. "Billy told me all about you and him and Cissy—"

"I can't deny what he told you. I'm just saying I didn't recognize either of them from the pictures you showed me." He turned to Karen. "We've talked about that since, and I don't deny the pictures. When you showed me the originals, of course I remembered. I just hadn't remembered their *faces*. I only saw them that one night. I still don't see what that has to do with Sarah's death—at least, I didn't until now. Now I think I'm beginning to understand.

"I didn't kill Sarah. I think that was always obvious—"

"Why is that obvious?" I asked.

"Because of you. You were the last one to see her, you saw her alive after I left her, you spent all that evening with me, and we found her dead together. I couldn't *possibly* have killed her. I thought a burglar had. But there is one other possibility."

"What?"

"That *you* killed her."

I glanced over at the *pizzella,* smiled at her. The last refuge of the scoundrel.

To my sudden horror, she didn't smile back.

Turner went on, talking to me. "Miss Douglass, Lieutenant Douglass, and I have been talking about it this evening. I couldn't have killed Sarah, but you could have.

While I waited out in the car, before we went to the movie. You could have killed her then."

"Ridiculous," I said. But I felt funny. To sit there and hear someone seriously accuse you of murder is a very funny feeling. You begin to sweat. Your voice sounds nervous. You can't help sounding guilty. "I had no reason to kill Sarah," I said. "I loved her."

The silence that followed that remark sounded ominous even to me. "I mean—" I began.

"We know what you mean," he said. "You loved her. So did I. We both loved her. But then she married me. And she was happy with me."

"She told me—"

"You've told us what you *say* she told you. Lieutenant Douglass tells me she has checked with several of our friends. None of them corroborates any statement of Sarah's that she was worried about me or frightened of me. Am I right? Is that correct?"

The *pizzella* nodded.

"So what do we really know?" he asked. "That we both loved Sarah. That she chose me. That we got married, and that you dropped out of sight. That suddenly you came back. And she was friendly. Of course she was, she loved you, I admit that. Only not as much as she loved me."

He waited for me to say something. I was silent.

"But," he said, "*but*, you crazy bastard, that was *years* ago. That was a different Sarah. That was *before* we got married." He sighed. "You never understood that, did you? You never understood that she *married* me, she *chose* me, because she *loved* me."

I glanced at the *pizzella*. Turner didn't know that I had been sleeping with Sarah during those last few weeks. Turner didn't know, but *she* knew. I had told her. And from the look in her eyes I could see that it only made Turner's nonsense sound more likely.

"This is crazy," I said.

"Crazy." He nodded. "You didn't understand that she didn't love you. Not enough to leave me. You stayed away for all those years because you couldn't get over her. Then you came back. I don't know, maybe you thought you *had* gotten over it. And then you saw her and you still loved her. Am I right?"

I didn't know what to say. He *was* right. . . .

"And she threw her arms around you and took you in, just like old times. Your love came flooding back and overwhelmed you, you probably made up in your mind how you'd ride off together on your white horse into the goddamn sunset. . . ."

He shook his head. "You were never in touch with reality," he said. "I don't know, maybe that's what you need to be a writer. A crazy imagination. And then what happened? Sarah said no, she wouldn't leave me. And you couldn't take that. You killed her."

"No," I said. "It didn't happen like that." I looked at the *pizzella*. She was sitting there quietly, listening to him as if he were making sense! "Listen," I said, "what happened in Miami *proves—*"

"Christ," Turner said. "Don't you see? Do you really not see what you've done? What happened in Miami fits right in! Who was the last person to see Sarah alive, the only person who had the chance to kill her? You. And who was the last person to see this guy Noel alive? You, goddamn it. *You!*"

"I wasn't the last person to see him alive—"

"Tell us about it," Douglass said. "Give us more details about last night."

"There isn't much more I can tell you," I said.
"Why not?"
"To tell you the truth, it's not that clear in my mind. We were drinking. I'd been drinking on the airplane down to Miami, and then after the show we sat around drinking beer. I talked with Noel, sure. I told you that. I don't actually remember leaving him. We were talking and drinking and then . . . I don't actually remember how the evening ended."

God, that sounded awful.

"Who sent you those pictures?" she asked.

The sudden turn in the question took me by surprise.

"You said it wasn't Noel," she said. "Who was it? Turner?"

"Cissy, I suppose."

"Why? Why would she do that?"

"I don't know."

"Did *anyone* send you the pictures?"

"What are you talking about? You *saw* them—"

"I'm not doubting their existence," she said. "I'm only wondering how you got them. Turner says his own copies are missing. Are those *his* copies you have? Did you find them in his house?"

"They came in the mail!"

"Anonymously?"

"Yes!"

"Why?"

I had no answer.

We sat in silence for a while.

Then Lieutenant Douglass stood up. "I don't think there's much more to discuss tonight."

"You can check on him," I said. "You can check with the airlines to see if he flew down to Miami yesterday."

"Yes, I'll do that."

"He could have bought the tickets under another name," I said.

"Yes, that's possible."

"And then you wouldn't know."

"It's possible."

"I'll bet no one saw him up *here* all day."

"That's true," Turner said. "I have no alibi. Thursday is my day for viewing properties. I drove down to Atlantic City and spent the day driving around, looking things over."

"You talked to people?"

"No. The place is disgusting since the mob took over. I decided against investing there. There was no reason to talk to anyone. I wasn't *planning* an alibi. But there will be no evidence that I flew down to Miami, because I didn't. On the other hand"—he glanced at me—"we know that you did. You're the only one who could have killed both Sarah and Noel."

"That would have been so stupid," I protested. I was talking to her. "You knew I was there, it would have been stupid to kill him. For *me* to kill him, I mean. And kill Sarah? When by my own admission I was the last one to see her alive? That would be *stupid*."

"Not stupid," Turner said quietly. "You said what it would be, you said it before. Not stupid," he said.

I looked at him.

"Crazy," he said.

Well, look, what can I tell you?
It's not true.
I am not a murderer. I am not crazy.

This is not going to be one of those books where the murderer turns out to be the narrator.

I didn't do it. Turner did.

You believe me, don't you?

CHAPTER 9

How did it get all turned around like that? All of a sudden Henry Grace, boy detective, had become Horrible Henry Grace the sex-crazed double murderer.

And I had to admit Turner's story made sense. It didn't make sense if you knew me, of course. It shouldn't have made sense to the *pizzella*, Lieutenant Karen Douglass, scourge of the underworld, tracer of lost persons, Brandeis graduate, and internationally renowned polo player who in the secret hills of Tibet discovered the lost power to cloud men's minds. . . . She should have known better.

I knew better.

But I stayed awake all night worrying about it.

The thing that bugged me, the thing that kept me awake all night, was that it *didn't* sound stupid. I mean, it should have been ludicrous, merely the *suggestion* that I could have done such a thing.

But it wasn't, was it? If Turner had killed Sarah, there were all kinds of problems. Like *when*, and *how*. If *I* had killed her, there was no problem. And motive? Well, Turner was closer there than he knew. I had loved her, but she certainly wasn't going to leave Turner for me, was she? I mean, even if I had asked her. Which I had not!

And Billy Noel. What had happened to Billy? I *know* I left him last night. It was after I left him that he had been . . . mugged? Whatever. At the time it happened I was probably lying drunk and asleep in Delmingo's pad. *Probably* . . .

Would Delmingo remember? Almost certainly not, he was further gone than I was. Christ, this was driving me crazy! . . .

I suppose I shouldn't have blamed the *pizzella* for deciding to think things over again, starting at square one. To her, Turner's story had to make sense.

I did a lot of pacing during this long night.

And it paid off. Because finally I cut through the fuzzy thinking and focused on the one thing that didn't make sense and also was amenable to further investigation: the photos. Damn it, I did *not* find those photos in Turner's house. Someone sent them to me. So all right, who?

Billy Noel had told me that only he, Cissy, and Turner had any of the snapshots. He hadn't sent them to me. It was a cinch Turner hadn't. Which left only Cissy.

And I was the only one who knew where Cissy was. They had interrupted me in the telling of my story last night. I had told them that I'd wanted to find Cissy before Turner killed her, and that was when the stuff hit the fan. I never did get around to telling them about the address left in her typewriter.

So it didn't take a great mind to figure out the next step. Even a schizophrenic psychopath like me could figure out the next step.

Find Cissy.

Okay, looking back on it now, I can see that maybe it wasn't such a great idea. Maybe the next step should have been to tell Police Lieutenant Douglass where Cissy was and let the cops go find her.

But not in a million years could I have done that. Not

the way I was feeling. Maybe I was stupid, but I was so angry at her that I had to do it *myself*. If she had been a man, I guess I wouldn't have been so upset. If she hadn't been so cool, so sure of herself, so rich, so goddamn superior!

If she hadn't so suddenly turned so cold toward me.

If she hadn't looked so cute.

Hell. I didn't admit any of this to myself. I just wanted to show her up, to bring her down.

So I went to find Cissy myself.

I took a series of buses to Watkins Glen, then another bus to Lake Charles. It took all day. Greyhound took Visa. I didn't know what Visa was going to take at the end of the month. Whatever I have left, I suppose. My blood. If Turner doesn't get it first.

One last bus got me into Diana's Trail at ten-thirty that night. The village of Diana's Trail, incorporated in the State of New York, consists of a general store cum post office on the highway, an abandoned service station, and a couple of roads leading away from the lake up into the hills. Across the highway, on the shore of the lake, a gravel road leads off into the trees. There's a little sign that points down that road. It says: "George's Rentals."

At ten-thirty at night the only indication of a surviving humanity is the lamplight shining in front of the general store. As the bus rumbled away down the highway and disappeared, as its sound dwindled and died, as the sounds of the trees in the breeze and the insects in the trees rose and took over the night, I felt definitely alone.

I stood on the highway and looked down the gravel road which *said* it went to George's Rentals. I didn't trust it. I stood safely in the civilized lamplight and peered down that road. Ten yards into it the trees shielded it and the light died. Twenty yards into it there was nothing but pitch blackness.

Well, what the hell. I left the highway and started down the road. I didn't really have any other choice.

It started to drizzle. From the moment I had stepped off the bus, I had never doubted that it would. I walked down the road and into the wet darkness. The trees were thick enough to cut off the light but not the rain. Somebody was awfully clever.

Within fifty yards I had actually to walk with my hands stretched out in front of my face to avoid walking off the road straight into a tree. Within a couple of hundred yards I decided to give up and go back. But then I thought, go back to what? There was nothing back there but an empty highway and the falling rain. I'd be dead of pneumonia by daybreak. And so, *excelsior*. That's how heroes are made.

The light appeared first as the tiniest flicker, like a firefly. As I walked onward it grew, blossomed, flared, and was finally revealed as an honest-to-God sixty-watt bulb on the wall of a shack.

The wall had a door beside the bulb and a sign below the bulb: "George's Rentals." Sing hallelujah hey nonny no, hey nonny no. . . .

I knocked.

"Who the hell's that!"

How do you answer that? If I call out, "Henry Grace," what's that going to mean? So how do you answer? "A wayfaring stranger? The highwayman?"

"Me," I said.

"Who the hell's me?" The door opened. An old, very thin man stood there. He stared at me. "Where'd the hell you come from?"

"The bus," I said.

"Walked down?"

I nodded.

"Why the hell didn't you call? Would have picked you up."

"I didn't see a phone."

He thought a moment. Then he nodded. "Ain't no phone," he agreed. "Well, come on in anyways."

I stepped in out of the drizzle. It was nearly as cold and damp inside. But only nearly, so I stepped in.

"What I mean," he said, "there's a phone in the store, but I guess that was closed."

I nodded.

"Yep," he said. "Help you?"

"I'm looking for someone. Cissy Massenick."

He stared at me blankly.

"Maybe twenty-five years old," I said. "Pretty girl—"

"Gorgeous girl," he said. "Yep, I know who you mean."

"She's here?"

"Yep."

"Alone?"

"Yep."

"No one else has come looking for her?"

He shook his head. He kept on shaking it, and after a while I understood that he was more than answering my question, he was commenting on the vagaries of humanity. "Knew there'd be someone," he said.

"What?"

"Knew there'd be someone comin' after her."

"Why?"

"Too pretty. Girl shouldn't be too pretty."

"But I'm the first? No one else has come."

"Tell you what, sonny," he said, putting his arm suddenly around my shoulder. "Tell you what you want to do. You want to go right back up that road and catch the next bus out of here, you hear me?"

"Why?"

"That girl's too pretty for you. A pretty girl is nothing but trouble. Now, you take me, I married the ugliest girl in this county, and I ain't never regretted it."

"Really?"

"Never regretted one day of it. Not even when a cute little piece like your girl comes walking in. No sir, never regretted one single day. And not one single night neither, if that's what you're thinking."

"I'm not thinking—"

"All cats are black in the night. What that means, it means you can't tell the difference when the light's out, you get that?"

"Yes, sir, I get it."

"Bernard Shaw said that."

"What?"

"Bernard Shaw, he wrote plays."

"Yes, I know—"

"*George* Bernard Shaw, most people call him. But he liked just Bernard. Good writer, too. No sir, I tell you, get yourself a plain woman. I never regretted it. What you smiling at?"

"It's just unusual to find someone who quotes Bernard Shaw anymore. Most people have forgotten him."

"Let me show you something." He pulled on my sleeve, he pulled me across the room to a door. He opened it, and there was another room, a small room piled high with books. Paperbacks, old books, stacked high. "Got 'em all in there," he said. "Shaw, Galsworthy, Christie, Harold Robbins, got 'em all. A lifetime of pleasure in that room. And you know what? Cost a damn sight less than a color television, all them books. And no monthly cable charge neither."

We stood there for a few moments admiring the books and thinking about life. Then I said, "Cissy Massenick?"

"You still want her? After all I told you?"

"Business," I said.

"Sure," he said.

"Where is she?"

"Out there."

"Where?"

He sighed. "You never been up here before?"

I shook my head.

"What we got here," he said, "is this lake, see? We got cabins all along the shore of this lake. She rented one of the cabins."

"Which one?"

He took me over to his desk, consulted his register, and drew me a map. "They ain't got numbers or addresses," he said.

"How do I get there?"

"You rent a canoe. And you paddle."

Oh, Christ.

"First thing in the morning," he said.

"I thought I'd go out tonight."

He shook his head. "Can't go out there tonight."

"Why not?"

"Look out there," he commanded, pointing through a window at pure blackness. "No lights out there. You'd never find it at night."

"I'd better try."

"Nope. Can't. Snakes'd get you."

"Snakes?" I began to feel crawly at that word.

He smiled. He could tell. "Snakes," he nodded. "Water

moccasins. Might walk right into one at night. Step out of the canoe and wham!"

I looked at him.

"Alligators, too," he said. "One gulp, that's all."

He was just trying to scare me.

Well, he wasn't just *trying*, if you get my meaning. But I was cold and wet and tired.

He smiled. A little smile. "Why don't you just stay the night at the motel?" he asked.

Oh, thank God. A motel. Visions of warmth and cleanliness and white sheets. I will never again sneer at Howard Johnson's. "Where's the motel?" I asked.

He smiled a great big smile. His hands spread wide. "This is it," he said.

I won't describe for you the room in which I spent the rest of the night, but do you remember Chapter Five of George Orwell's *Down and Out in Paris and London*? At any rate, as the Good Book tells us, all things pass, and so too did the night.

There was no need to pull back the curtains the next morning to look outside. For one thing, there weren't any curtains. For another, you couldn't see anything outside anyhow. The world was bathed in a soft gray fog. Somewhere up above there must have been a sun, but you couldn't tell from down here. The light came through weakly, diffuse, from all directions, and all it showed you was the soft gray fog pitter-pattering through the woods.

It thinned out a bit after breakfast—I won't describe breakfast—and the old man took me down to the lake shore. He held the canoe while I climbed into it, and gave me a push to start me on my way across the flat glass surface of the gray lake.

The way I viewed the situation, it was like this. Either

I killed Sarah without knowing it, or I didn't. Either I'm a psychopath or I'm not. I say I'm not. But if you're really a psycho, do you know it? Of course not. In fact, that's sort of a precondition to *being* one. It's Catch-22: if you *think* you're sane, maybe you're not. You might even say that anyone who thinks he's sane in this world *must* be nuts.

So how do you tell?

Well, I don't know about you, but I knew how I could tell. The photos. If this girl Cissy says she sent them to me, and if they throw some light on how Turner killed Sarah, then I'm home clean.

Of course, if she says she *didn't* send them to me . . . But I know I didn't take them from Turner's house! I swear I remember getting them in the mail! If only I had saved the envelope . . .

Never mind.

Talk to Cissy. She'll tell me about the photos. I'm *sure* she will.

The shore of the lake is a jigsaw puzzle of coves. Because of the fog I couldn't steer straight down the center of the lake but had to stay within fifteen or twenty yards of the zigzagging shore, following the meandering shoreline in and out, checking off landmarks and cabins against the map the old man had drawn.

There was no sign of life. This early in the year the lake was deserted. She could have had any cabin she wanted. I wondered why she hadn't simply taken the closest. But I suppose the whole point of coming to a place like this, just slightly beyond the ends of the earth, is to get away.

So I paddled for nearly two hours before I finally pulled into her particular cove. It was hard work, paddling like that, and I was sweating under my arms and down my back by the time I reached her. The fog and the lake breeze were cold. I was coming down with pleurisy and the ague, and I was sick and disgusted with myself for having made this unnecessary trip.

I paddled the canoe up to the shore. I couldn't see any way of getting out of it without stepping into at least a few inches of water. I looked around at the water carefully, very carefully. I didn't see any water moccasins. Or alligators.

I stepped out into the ankle-deep water. I had always thought that water froze when the temperature dipped to zero degrees. I was wrong.

I pulled the canoe up on the grass and walked up the slope to the cabin.

"Cissy?" I called.

There was no answer. The sweat under my armpits was turning cold. My ankles were gone. I banged on the door. "Cissy?" I called again.

I might have the wrong cabin, I thought. If I did, how would I ever find the right one? I'd have to go back to the old man and start all over again. I might never find the right one.

Or maybe this was the right one. Maybe Cissy was inside, but in no mood to answer. Maybe Cissy was in no condition to answer. Maybe Cissy was even colder than I was, but not feeling it. Maybe Cissy was dead.

She opened the door.

You know, I think maybe I *am* crazy. All those times I had been looking at those Polaroid snapshots, I had really been looking only at Turner. It took me by surprise, seeing how beautiful she was. I hadn't noticed. She was wearing old jeans and a gray sweat shirt, and oh, I hate to be the one to tell the ladies of this world that all the millions of dollars they spend each year on Dior and Cardin and Gucci and Berger Christensen and Formfit could be given to the starving children of India for all the good it's doing the ladies. Clothes do *not* make you beautiful, ladies, makeup doesn't make you beautiful. If you've got it, kid, you've got it. And if you don't, cultivate your mind or take up rug-weaving or Zen, because there's nothing you can do, there's nothing you can buy, there's nothing you can put on that can make you look like Cissy. In old jeans and a rumpled sweat shirt.

She smiled.

I just stood there and stared at her. How can I explain? Look, it was just—night before last I had the *pizzella* clawing my back, right? All of a sudden from out in left field she decided I was a psychopath, right? As a result of which I spent all day yesterday on the bus, from New York City to Watkins Glen to Lake Charles and Diana's Trail, right?

Now, you may not be able to imagine what it's like suddenly to be accused of being a psychopathic sex murderer, that's probably outside of your recent field of experience. But with a little imagination you ought to be able to visualize what it feels like to spend all day on buses. And then to be dropped off at Diana's Trail with no place to rest your head or escape from the drizzle except George's Rentals.

And then, to cap it all off, just imagine spending two hours on a cold, foggy lake, paddling until your arms fall out of their sockets. And then, after all this, to have a dirty cabin door suddenly open and see that face in front of you. Smiling at you.

It's just too much.

My locomotor reflex system just couldn't handle it.

I stood there and stared at her.

Skin white and soft. High cheekbones, mildly slanted eyes. There was a towel wrapped around her head, with wisps of jet black hair slipping out of it. And a smile that dispelled the fog and the cold, that lit up all the outdoors. Was this the face that launched a thousand ships, and burnt the topless towers of Ilium? O sweet Cissy, make me immortal with a kiss. . . .

She laughed at the expression on my face, and I could have knelt down and wept for joy.

"Well, where'd you come from, then?" she asked.

It was time to break the spell. "It's a long story," I said. "My name is Henry Grace—"

Her eyes widened. "Not *the* Henry Grace?" she asked. "The playwright?"

And I loved her from that moment on.

Well, okay, I got carried away. That was the first time anyone had ever said that to me, the first time anyone had ever recognized my name. I'm assuming, in saying that, that someday there will be a second time. It's got to be like the first time you ever went to bed with a girl. No matter *who* she is, you're going to love her forever. Or at least until the second time.

So.

Cissy Massenick.

Aside from being probably the world's most beautiful girl, Cissy Massenick is an actress. Now, you understand I had never seen her act, but from what I *had* seen of her I'd have had to say that she must be a rather terrible actress. Because with that face and body, if she weren't absolutely terrible she would be a star. (To become a star, you have to be neither more nor less than just a little bit terrible. Of course, after you have become a star you can get as terrible as you like. At that point it even helps. They call it *personality*.)

She took me into the kitchen and gave me fresh coffee and homemade bread for breakfast. Homemade bread, can you imagine? And she chattered on about her acting career. It was the weirdest sensation. I had never met this girl before in my life, and here I was appearing out of nowhere by the shores of Gitche Gumee, and she recognizes me and brings me into her kitchen and plies me with fresh coffee and homemade bread and chatters away at me like I was her kid brother.

I was very happy.

But she does have a problem.

She was, as I thought, a rather terrible actress. (When an old actress admits she's still learning, that's a sign that she's a very good actress. When a young actress admits the same thing, you know she's been told so many times that she doesn't know a damned thing about technique that it's beginning to sink in.)

So she's been having a rough time finding work. She gets auditions easily enough—anyone glancing at her is sure to ask her to read—but the catch is that then she *does* have to read the lines.

She smiled that fantastic smile. All those white teeth. And more than that, a smile that just *begins* with those white teeth, that spreads up over those fantastic cheekbones into those dark brown eyes—oh, my God. . . .

She smiled and said, "And then after I read I don't get the part." She shrugged. "At least, not very often. But I *want* to be an actress."

And so does half the population of Peoria. Which makes it difficult to get work, even if you're a good actress. Which she is not, and there you are.

On the other hand, she has this other offer. There is this guy down in Miami who has used her in a couple of movies and who thinks she has that charismatic *je ne sais quoi* that is known in the profession (in tribute to an early director) as "zee star quality." And so, naturally, he wants to sign her to a contract and make her a star.

"Well, that's great," I told her. "In the movies you don't *have* to act. Go be a star."

She shrugged. "I don't know," she said.

"It sounds good to me," I said.

"Well," she said, "but you know? These movies he wants me to make, they're not exactly your normal family entertainment. You know?"

I was beginning to get the picture. I'm not so slow. "Porno films?" I asked.

She nodded. "He says I can be bigger than Marilyn Chambers. The money will be good."

"I never knew money that was bad. Do you like making those movies?"

She nodded. Enthusiastically. "I really do," she said. "I'm not acting. I can be a good actress," she said ruefully, "if I'm not acting."

So anyhow, that was why she had come up here. To get away from things, get away from this guy in Miami, think things out. The age-old problem: suffer for your art, or grab the quick buck? I can't think of one other profession in which anyone would even think twice. There's not one insurance man, not one dentist, not one engineer or truck driver or hackie or football player that would hesitate for a moment. But she was serious. Should she spend the next twenty years trying to learn her profession properly so that when she's fifty she could *maybe* give a good performance of Juliet's nurse, or should she grab the easy money now?

"So," she said. "What shall I do?"

I started to smile in sympathy, then realized it was not a rhetorical question. She was asking *me*. She expected an answer.

"Hey," I said, "I don't know." I wasn't about to take responsibility for the rest of her life. I didn't feel ready to take responsibility for the rest of *my* life.

She leaned her head to one side. She seemed to be unconscious of the grace of her movements. "Why did you come here?" she asked.

Well, that was a bit awkward, wasn't it? But I had to tell her sooner or later. "I was looking for you—" I began.

"No," she interrupted. "You're wrong."

"You haven't heard what I was going to say."

"It doesn't matter. What I mean is that you *can't* be right, you can't understand why you came here."

"All right then, I bite. Why did I come here?"

"For me. You're part of my fate, my karma. I have to make this decision, and I don't know what to do. So you were sent to help me."

"Me?"

"Who else? You're the best new playwright in the world, you understand the stage better than—"

"Hey, hold on, I'm not."

"You are! I saw *Courtesy*. I'd rather have your advice than anyone's. Except maybe Tennessee Williams'," she added. She thought a moment. "Or—"

"Hey, don't ruin it," I said.

We looked at each other.

She waited.

"No," I said. "I can't help you. I don't know you, I haven't seen you work. I can't tell you what to do."

"I could read for you?"

I shook my head. I can't straighten out my own life, how am I going to help with hers? "I'm sorry," I said.

"Oh well," she said with a sigh, "never mind, then. If you can't, you can't. At least we can make love."

"What?"

"I've been here all by myself for two weeks," she explained. "You aren't gay?"

"No," I said.

"That's settled, then. But first we'll hike?"

"Hike? You mean outside?"

"That's what we do on Lake Charles. We fish or canoe or hike or swim. It's probably too cold for you to go swimming, isn't it?"

"It's too cold for *seals* to go swimming."

She laughed. "I've been swimming every day, that's why I came all the way up here from Miami. Want to give it a try? Jump in the icy water and then bake out in front of the fire?"

"You must be crazy."

"Sort of," she admitted. "Swedish, on my mother's side. I don't suppose you have any Viking blood in you?"

"Not a drop."

"Then we'll just have to hike," she decided.

So we hiked. The fog was beginning to lift, but it was still cold and wet and the ground was muddy. For the first hour I was chilled and miserable. Then the ground began to slope upward and the going got harder and I began to sweat, and so for the second hour I was hot and miserable. The third hour wasn't so bad, because we turned around and were headed home. The fourth hour was unmitigated hell. We were lost.

It's all woods, thick woods. You can't hike along the shore of the lake because there it's all muddy and swampy and that's where the snakes live, she explained. So we had hiked inland away from the lake, and now the trees seemed to be getting thicker no matter which way we turned. I was starting to panic as the light began to fade. There wasn't all that much light anyhow here in the woods, and I didn't want to be caught in here when the sun went down and the animals came out. Did the snakes know they were supposed to stay down by the lake?

All right, laugh, I'm a city boy.

"I'm not laughing," she laughed.

I remembered something from *Boy's Tales.* "You're supposed to mark a trail when you go hiking in the woods," I said.

"Yes," she agreed. "That would have been a good thing to do."

"There must be other people around."

"Where?"

"Somewhere! We could shout?"

She shook her head. "I've been here two weeks," she said, "and you're the only person I've seen. The season doesn't really start until summer."

"Help!" I yelled.

She stopped and put her hands on her hips. "We're not really lost, you know."

"You could have fooled me."

"Didn't you really notice that all the way up from the cabin we kept the lake on our left? So now it has to be down there on the right. If we keep on this way we have to come out somewhere on the shoreline—"

"Where the snakes are."

"They won't hurt you."

"Water moccasins?"

She shrugged as if I had a point, which did *not* reassure me. She shrugged, and started off. I wanted to call her back, but then what? We couldn't stay here. I followed her.

It was getting darker. It was getting harder to see. It was getting harder to see faster than it was getting darker. At first I didn't notice, then I thought something was going wrong with my eyes. Then I realized what it was. "It's not getting foggy again, is it?" I asked her.

"The fog always comes down at night," she called over her shoulder. "It's something to do with spring. There it is!"

"What?"

"The lake."

She waited for me to catch up, and pointed through the trees. With the best will in the world, I couldn't call the patch of darkness that was all I could see a lake. But she was sure of herself.

"That's it," she said complacently. "So we're all right now."

"The snakes," I suggested.

"We'll just stay up here on high ground and walk parallel to the lake shore. We'll just keep it in sight."

I didn't point out to her that it wasn't in my sight. She started walking, and I just followed her, and we were home in not much more than another half hour.

We walked into the cabin. I made a particular effort not to stagger. She didn't seem at all tired. She lit an oil lamp. She asked if I'd like a beer. I looked around the cabin. There was no electricity, no refrigerator. But even warm, even American beer, I'd take anything.

She went out in the darkness, and came back a couple of moments later with two wet bottles of McEwan's. "The lake's a natural refrigerator," she said.

I sank back into the one chair and took a long drink. She sat on the bed. "You don't have any luggage," she said.

I nodded. "I didn't plan this trip out right," I admitted.

She took a long drink. "Your socks will be stinking by now," she said.

I wiggled my toes. My shoes were soaked, and inside

them my socks were worse. Yes, they'd be stinking by now. And my shirt was damp with sweat and my underpants—

"You'd better get all your clothes off," she said. "I'll wash them out for you in the lake."

"I'll do it," I said.

"You'd better let me."

"Why?"

"The snakes."

I didn't know if everyone was kidding me about the snakes or not. But what the hell, if she wanted to wash out the clothes . . .

I took them off. She sat on the bed and drank her beer and watched me. I took off my shoes and socks, and then my shirt. I felt like Gypsy Rose Lee. I took off my pants and underpants.

She got off the bed and knelt in front of me and picked up the pile. She took them out the door.

It was cold. I was damp with perspiration. I found a towel and rubbed myself dry. I rubbed harder, trying to get warm. I wondered if it would be polite to get into bed. I know I'm the sophisticated New York playwright—*the* Henry Grace, after all—but I didn't feel very sophisticated. I didn't know what was coming. I was also getting hungry. And I had to ask her about the pictures, I had forgotten all about that. I had forgotten why I had come up here in the first place. I was cold and hungry and—

She came back in, carrying the wet clothes. Hers and mine. She came back in stark naked. And suddenly I wasn't cold and hungry anymore.

She draped them over the chair and then padded in her bare feet to a corner of the room and bent down. "I'll make us a fire," she said. I hadn't noticed the small fireplace. In just a few moments she had it blazing. She padded back across the room, kissed me lightly on the cheek, and got into bed. She sat up primly in the bed and folded her hands neatly across her belly.

"Now then," she said.

The fire had died down to a warm, cheery glow. I had fallen asleep. No, not fallen. Slipped. Sleep was a soft big white cotton ball, and I was slipping in and out like a glider bouncing on the edge of a puffy white cloud.

She scratched my back. I sailed lightly out of the cloud and opened my eyes. The room was warm and cozy and I felt so *good*.

"Hungry?" she asked.

I felt so good I didn't want to talk or move, afraid it would go away. I smiled. She got out of bed. "I dropped some lines in," she said, "when I did the washing. I'll see if anything bit."

I didn't know what she was talking about. I didn't care. I just lay there and watched her float across the room and out the door into the night.

I was half-asleep still, half-dreaming, and she came back into our cabin with the low, cheery light of the fire flickering over her skin as my lips had done—

She was carrying a fish. She held it up for me to see.

"We got one," she said. She took a frying pan out of the dark corner and put the fish on the table and went swish with a knife and then bent over the open fire and the fish began to sizzle and fill the cabin with its aroma. I wondered if I had somehow died and gone to heaven.

And then I remembered that I hadn't. Someone else had died. I found my wallet and opened it and took out the Polaroid snapshot that I'd brought along to show her.

It was there in my wallet, all right, and I was still here on earth where people killed people.

I was awake now. I sat naked at the table and waited for her to finish frying the fish.

"We're out of beer," she said as she attended to the fire, "but there's some coffee left. I'll heat it up."

There was a thin line of sweat on her lip from the heat of the fire as she laid our food on the table. A thin trickle ran down from her neck and up and across one breast. I reached across the table and wiped it away with a finger. We smiled at each other and took our first bite of the world's most delicious fish and I pushed the Polaroid across the table and asked, "Do you know these guys?"

She glanced down at it. "I forgot the bread," she said, and jumped up. She brought back the remainder of the homemade bread we had had that morning. "We're out of butter," she said, and sat down. She looked at the picture again. "Do I know them? Are you kidding?"

"Who are they?"

"That's Turner and Billy. Where'd you get the picture?"

"Didn't you send it to me?"

She cocked her head on one side as she had done when I had first told her I couldn't advise her on what to do with her life. "How could I send it to you?" she asked. "I don't know you."

I didn't believe her.
I didn't *believe* she had said that.
I looked across the table at her. She was bending over her plate, eating her fish, unaware of the importance of her words. Unaware that she was sitting there naked supping with a psychopathic murderer. A schizo. A Dr. Jekyll and Mr. Hyde type.

I was scared.

If she hadn't sent me the photos, *where had they come from?* If she hadn't sent me the photos, *who had killed Sarah?* Turner? Or—

I took another bite of the fish. I drank the coffee.

"Billy or Turner must have sent you the picture," she said. "They're the only ones who have any."

I looked at her. She sucked on a fish bone. She smiled at me.

She was not lying.

For one thing, why should she lie? If she *had* sent the photos, why deny it? For another, I *knew* she was not lying like I knew Turner had killed Sarah, I saw it in her face.

I tried to smile back at her.

Would I kill her too?

Maybe it was something like rabies, maybe it was something inside me that took control and I never remembered—

I shook my head violently.

"What is it?" she asked.

"Nothing. Tell me about them. About Billy and Turner."

She swallowed. "Billy's an actor down in Miami, you know." I nodded. "Very good-looking, but not much else. Competent onstage, competent in bed, fun at a party. Not much else. Typical provincial actor. I don't mean to sound snotty, he's better than I am, but I can *recognize* good acting even if I can't—"

I nodded. I had been so sure that Cissy was going to be the key that would unlock the mystery. I had been *sure* that she was going to tell me how Turner had committed the impossible murder.

"There's more to Turner," she said. "I mean, he's more

as a human being. He used to be an actor, but he's in some kind of business now. I met him last summer when I was working in dinner theater upstate. Florida, I mean. He was down for a weekend and he knew the stage manager and we went out together and we became friends. He's quiet, but a wild one, you know." She began to chuckle. "He's funny, Turner."

"How close are you?"

She shrugged. "*Comme ci, comme ça.* He's come down a few times. To Miami, I mean. Nothing serious." She smiled brightly. "Just good friends. He seems the serious type, but inside he's very funny. When you really know him."

We finished the fish, sipped the last of the coffee. "What do you mean," I asked, "funny?"

She gave a little giggle. Then she shook her head. "No," she said. "I really shouldn't tell you."

"You don't mean queer funny? Crazy funny?"

"Oh no," she said, "nothing like that. He's as straight as they come. I meant ha-ha funny. Like practical jokes, you know?"

I didn't know. I didn't remember Turner as a jokester. But it didn't matter. He hadn't killed Sarah for laughs. Nothing mattered. Nothing she could say mattered. What do I do now? That was what I was thinking. Where do I go from here?

"He went to incredible lengths for a joke," she was saying. I wasn't listening. I wasn't interested in jokes.

"It wasn't you, was it?" she was asking. "That we played that joke on? Did you know his wife?"

I wasn't really listening.

"Is there any more coffee?"

She shook her head. "Did you know his wife?" she asked again.

"Yes. Why? Did you know her?"

"Oh no. I was just wondering if it was you we played that joke on."

"What joke?"

She started to answer, then clapped her hand across her mouth. "No, I really mustn't tell you. That's the whole point of a practical joke, you mustn't ever tell. I promised Turner."

Something clicked. I leaned forward. I asked the most important question of my life. I asked quietly, "Cissy, what was the joke?"

"I really shouldn't tell you. Especially if it was you we played it on."

"Cissy, please. What was the joke about?"

She gave a little smile in surrender.

"About murdering Turner's wife," she said.

"It was a few months ago," she said.

"December," I said.

"Yes."

"December tenth."

She gave a little gasp. "Oh, it *was* you."

I was beginning to realize what had happened. "I think you'd better tell me the whole story," I said.

"Have you been worrying about it ever since?"

"The whole story, Cissy. Please."

She bit her lip in contrition. She nodded her head. "All right." She paused to think about it. "It *sounded* funny when he told me," she said.

"Cissy. Just tell me, huh?"

Another nod. "I flew up from Miami. Turner paid, of course. I thought that was terribly expensive just for a joke, but he said that a really good joke is like a work of art. Like a stage production. A lot of good plays have closed after just one night, that doesn't make the effort put into them less worth while, he said. He was very serious about it."

"What was the joke, Cissy?"

"He had a friend staying with him for the weekend. I suppose that was you? He said it was his best friend. His wife was sick, I think she had had some teeth pulled. At any rate, she would be dosed up with sleeping pills and would be knocked out. He was going to get his friend—you—out of the house on some pretext or other. A movie or something like that. I would be waiting down the street.

"I had come in that afternoon, you see, and he had reserved a car for me at Kennedy—he paid for that too—and then I drove up and was waiting down the street from the house that evening. He went out to get the car ready while his friend—while you—were still in the house with his wife. He drove around to the front door and honked and you came out and got in and drove away with him."

I nodded.

"After you had left, I put on these men's shoes he had given me and walked across the grass into the house. He had left a door open for me, you know that glass door that leads into his den?"

"Why the men's shoes?"

"I didn't really get that. He said he might want to carry the joke further, and I should wear them just in case. Anyway. There was plenty of time, so I just relaxed in his den. I read *Two Mondays*. The Arthur Miller? God, I'd love to do that. Agnes? Do you know the part? It's not a big part but there's so much *to* it. Not many playwrights know how to write women's parts. Aside from Tennessee—"

"Cissy. Tell me what happened."

"Well, about eleven o'clock, about an hour and a half later, I knew you'd be coming back soon, so I put on the blond wig and the blue bathrobe he had given me. I lay down on the floor in front of the desk. And I waited."

"We came in and saw you there. I thought you were Sarah."

She nodded. "You were supposed to. Oh, and I had left the glass door open, you remember that?"

"Yes. It looked like a burglar had come in."

"The idea was, you were supposed to get scared and run off to the police and tell them a murder had been done and when you brought them back Turner would be sitting there quietly watching television and Sarah would be safely asleep upstairs. He'd pretend he didn't know anything about it, and they'd think it was *you* trying to play a joke on *them*."

That son of a bitch. That bastard.

"It sure *sounded* like you were scared. It was a terrible temptation to try to sneak a look. But of course that would have ruined everything. Then after you left Turner came back in the room and told me and I just walked back out to the car—"

"In the men's shoes?"

"Right. And I left. I drove back in to the city, where I had arranged to stay with some friends. And then I drove out to Connecticut—Turner said I could keep the rental car for a few days, he's a sport, Turner—and I had a nice little vacation and then I flew back to Miami. And that's it."

And that was it. It hit me hard. It felt as if someone had physically punched me in the stomach, knocking out my breath. This vision of Turner actually killing Sarah. This vision of Turner standing in the doorway, calmly watching me race away down the road to get the cops. This vision of Turner breaking one of the panes in the glass door. Then going upstairs. Waking Sarah. Bringing her downstairs into the den.

Slitting her throat.

And then waiting for the police with a perfect alibi.

I had always known it, had always known he must have done it. But it had been an idea, nothing more. Nothing real.

This vision was real. It was so real I could see him with the knife, I could hear her screaming. . . .

It staggered me. And like a phantasmagoria of swirling nightmares other visions came pouring in on me, spinning me around. Visions past, present, and future.

Vision of the present: this lovely lady sitting across the table from me, smiling shamefacedly as she tells me how she contrived with Turner to murder my Sarah, not understanding that she is talking of real murder.

Vision of the past: her lovely smile twisting into Turner's wicked grinning face, her clasped fingers folding into Sarah's, her voice fading into Sarah's voice pleading, begging, finally screaming. . . .

Vision of the future: Turner, rising from Sarah's body, from the smoke of the fire, from the fog off the lake, Turner rising suddenly before us in this room to kill us both. For kill us he must.

I shook my head violently.

"What is it?" she asked. "What's wrong?"

My stomach was heaving. I thought I was going to be physically sick with fear. "Where's the bathroom?" I asked.

She laughed. "Out there. There's a trail outside the cabin."

I lurched out. "Here," she said, handing me a flashlight. "Are you all right?"

I found the trail, I found the outhouse, I was sick. The smell was disgusting. The joys of nature fade away when the digestive system backfires. There are definitely things to be said for civilization.

I stood outside the outhouse and leaned against a tree. Upwind. With the easing of my physical sickness the fear that had brought it on also seemed to fade. It didn't disappear, it was there, but it was no longer overwhelming, incapacitating. I could think about it.

The more I thought, the better it seemed. Turner actually had murdered Sarah, all right. He had conned Cissy into what she had thought was a joke, to give him an alibi. He had thought that she would never hear of what had happened to his wife. It was a cinch it wouldn't make the Miami papers, with more than two hundred of their own homicides to sell papers with. There seemed no way that anyone investigating Sarah's murder would ever hear of Cissy.

But then someone had sent me the pictures. Who? I didn't know. Never mind. I had dug up Cissy.

And Turner knew that I had. I told him two nights ago that I had found Billy Noel, that I knew Cissy's name and Miami address.

So Turner had to kill Cissy. Q.E.D.

He had to kill her before she told anyone about the joke.

Too late. She had already told me. So he had to kill me too.

But wait. He didn't know that she had told me. He didn't know that I had found her. *He didn't even know where she was!*

So we were safe after all.

Right out here, alone on this lake, we were the safest people in the world.

There was no need to panic. I could take my time and think it out. What we could do is call the *pizzella* and tell her the story and have her arrest Turner on the spot, and then with him safely in jail we could wander on home at our leisure.

It was too late tonight. Too late to canoe in to the office of George's Rentals and use the phone. But no hurry. Tomorrow would do fine. Tonight I could relax with Cissy.

That didn't sound like a bad idea. I wouldn't tell her the whole story yet. Women are prone to panic. I wouldn't tell her anything until after I had called the *pizzella* and Turner was safely in jail and there would be nothing for her to be afraid of.

I turned on the flashlight and looked for the trail. Even with the light, it was hard to find. Pitch black in these woods thick with trees. But I found it all right, and came back to the cabin.

"Are you all right?" she asked.

She had pulled the bedclothes off the bed and laid them out in front of the fire. She was stretched out there with the glow of the fire playing over her body.

She stretched like a cat in the fire's warmth, purred, and smiled, and just as I was about to leap she said, "I'd like to read for you."

Oh no, I thought. I shook my head. If you read for me I'll have to tell you what I honestly think, and that will be the end of our lovely evening. I can lie about many things. If a girl's a Republican, as I fondle her I can say that Ford was a great President. If the girl's a moron, I think I could even say that Nixon was a great Presi— No, I can't *quite* say that. But I *can* lie about many things. Many things—but not the stage. Not acting. I'll tell you the truth, my love, and then spend the rest of the evening watching you sulk.

She stood up. "I'm going to read for you," she said.

I sighed. "Put something on," I said.

"What?"

"Put something on. I can't concentrate with a naked

woman standing in front of me. I'm funny that way."

She swept up the sheet from the bed and swirled it around her. "Amanda," she announced. "*Glass Menagerie?*"

I nodded and settled down to watch. At least she hadn't picked *Same Time Next Year* or *Prisoner of Second Avenue* or, God forbid, Lady Macbeth. She wasn't stupid, this girl. So how was I going to tell her—

"'I can see the handwriting on the wall as plain as the nose on my face,'" she read. "'It's terrifying! More and more you remind me of your father! He was out all hours without explanation—then left! Good-bye! And me with the bag to hold. I saw that letter you got from the Merchant Marine. I know what you're dreaming—'"

"No," I said.

She stopped and looked at me.

"Don't use your eyes," I said. "Amanda doesn't have eyes like yours."

I expected an argument, but she just nodded and went on. Without taking my eyes off her, fascinated and surprised, I reached out and found a paper bag—a used grocery bag—on the table. I began to jot down notes. Because there was so much wrong with her—and because there was so much *good*.

She wasn't ready for Amanda, Amanda is one of the very few truly magnificent women's roles, she wasn't within twenty years of being ready for Amanda, but this beautiful naked lady with the sheet wrapped nearly around her was an *actress*. She was raw, she was undisciplined, I could see why no one hired her. I wouldn't hire her myself, not yet. But inside that gorgeous body there was an *actress* straining at the seams. As she read, as she swirled around and took center stage in this cabin in the woods, I got more and more excited. And when she finished—

"'Laura, come here and make a wish on the moon. A little silver slipper of a moon. Look over your left shoulder, Laura, and make a wish! Wish for happiness! And good fortune. . . .'"

When she finished and stood in front of me looking vainly for that misbegotten moon, I knew I had found something. I had so much to tell her, I didn't know where to begin.

She stood still for a moment, then hugged the sheet tightly around her for protection and turned away from me, toward the fire. "I'll put us on some coffee," she said.

I nodded, searching for the right words.

Her back was turned. She couldn't see the expression on my face. "You don't have to say anything," she said. "Please don't feel you have to be polite. You can stop searching for something noncommittal to say. You wouldn't fool me anyhow. I just wanted to read for you, I didn't expect any—"

"Watch your hands," I said, looking at the brown paper bag, twisting and turning it to find where I had started. "You have a dancer's hands, but you indulge them. When you say, 'I'm old and don't matter,' you've got a nice gesture. But it ruins that perfect toss of the wrist on 'Put your wool muffler on!' You can't do both. You've got to set them up with immobility, then *crush* them at the right time."

She stood there, staring at me. She nodded.

"Don't be afraid to talk softly. Don't be afraid to whisper. Not too suddenly, you have to draw us in so we strain to hear you. When you say, for example . . ."

She came back to me and sank down on the floor. She wrapped her arms around her knees. She nodded, she listened, and I talked on and on. I had a dozen notes for her and twice two dozen more things to say that I hadn't had time to write down. They tumbled around in my head and came spilling and splashing out. I must have talked for an hour, maybe more.

Finally I stopped. I looked down at her. She hadn't moved. There was still so much more to tell her, but it would have to wait. "Just one more thing," I said.

She waited.

"You're not an actress. Not yet. You couldn't get up on a stage tomorrow and make people believe that you're Amanda, that you're lonely and frustrated and yearning for your youth, for your father, for the love and comfort of your family, that you're helpless and torn by your daughter's—oh hell, you know all that."

"Yes."

"You're not an actress. But I'll tell you this, you're damn well *going* to be an actress. And you are good and goddamned well told *not* going to be a porno queen. Say good-bye to all that lovely money. Say good-bye to the fast and easy life."

"Good-bye," she said.

"Say hello to me," I said.

"Hello," she said. "You."

She didn't need the sheet for protection anymore, and it had slipped down.

"Get into bed," she said. "I'll make us some fresh coffee."

"I can't drink coffee at night," I said. "I'll stay awake all night."

She stood up and the sheet fell away. She smiled wickedly. She dropped her voice so that she drew me in, so that I had to lean forward and strain to hear. "Good," she said.

Curtain.

Wild applause.

CHAPTER 10

Morning.
There was no sudden bolt of sunlight through the unshaded windows to shock a man into waking, but rather a slow and dim burgeoning of the consciousness of light. A gentle end to a brilliantly long and energetic night.

I was not yet awake, but already I knew I was happy. I stretched and groaned with the last of my sleep, and I didn't yet know *why* I was happy. I kept my eyes closed and stretched and yawned, and slowly I remembered.

I opened my eyes. She wasn't there. I leaned up on one elbow to look out the window for her, but the world out there was blanketed in fog. The white lake fog. It swirled up from the water and twisted through the trees and settled over the cabin and sealed the windows in white. I couldn't even see the outhouse, not even the trail to it.

No matter. I hopped out of bed and flung the window wide open and the wispy fog blew gently, coldly, into the room, swirling around my curled toes. No matter. This was my evocation of the Viking spirit. But enough is enough. I took one deep, cold breath and then hopped right back into bed and pulled the covers up around my chin. The warmth of her body was still trapped in these covers and the bed was soft and warm and now only the tip of my nose was cold. I smiled and huddled down in the covers and closed my eyes.

I slept.

I woke again, and I was still alone. This time my eyes popped open as soon as I realized that I had again slept, that time had passed, that the cabin was still empty.

I sat up. Could Turner somehow have . . . ?

I jumped out of bed. She wasn't here. I opened the door. Nothing but the white fog. I couldn't even see the lake. "Cissy!" I called. The shout disappeared into the fog.

I came back into the cabin and looked around. She wasn't here. What could have—

There was a note on the pillow, the pillow next to mine. "*Salud, macho!* No bread, no coffee, no makin's. Gone to fetch them. Back in a trice. Sleep, my love. Sleep."

I laughed. With relief, and with love.

Well, I didn't know. To tell the truth, I had this funny feeling that I wanted to tell the *pizzella* all about it, and that confused me. At any rate, I had found something here on the foggy shore of this lost lake in upstate New York. I had found something important, and I wasn't going to let her go.

I flopped down on the bed, the better to think. I rolled over and over and back and forth, and I thought about her. I remembered her. I began to anticipate her return.

I heard the soft slurp of a paddle in the water. I stood quietly, listening, and heard the little sigh of a canoe nudging in to shore. She'd be coming up the path in another moment. I knew she wouldn't be naked, but that's how I visualized her, that's how I'll always think of her. I stood up and my manhood, as they say in those slightly risqué Victorian novels, jutted stiffly out in front of me.

I laughed. I have always thought of men as ugly, hairy, obscene creatures. But now, like Richard the Third, I thought myself to be a marvelous proper man. I must be lovely, if she doth think me so. Could such a creature as she, a creature of beauty pure and simple, could such a creature love something that is not itself beautiful? Oh, say not so! Ergo, I must be beautiful, though I never thought so.

There were steps outside, slow and heavy in the fog. Heavy bundles, I thought, coffee and beer and flour for fresh bread. But first we'll feast on love. For I am beautiful! In her beauty is mine own body transmogrified—

The door creaked open and I stood there with my manhood erect and my arms thrown open to receive her. "Look," I cried, "I am beautiful!"

The door opened wide.

"Gorgeous," Turner said.

CHAPTER 11

Talk about your phallic symbols. I stood there, shocked into catatonia, my authentic and original phallic symbol clutched withering in my hand. Turner stepped into the room clutching his own phallic symbol, thrusting it before him—a sawed-off shotgun. Twin-barreled.

He held his symbol leveled directly at mine.

I backed away, bumped into the bed, and sat down hard.

He stood there and smiled at me. He wore a long overcoat, and a muffler hung loosely around his neck. The hands that held the gun wore black leather gloves. He stood there, breathing deeply. He smiled.

"Where is she?" he asked.

"Who?"

"Don't play games!" He was suddenly angry, hissing, snarling, threatening. "Where is she?"

I was too shocked to answer. It seemed as if he would burst with his fury. He raised the gun toward me, held it out stiffly and awkwardly in both gloved hands. It was all the more terrible for the awkwardness. I was suddenly sweating. Cold sweat. I shivered uncontrollably. I was terrified. I thought he was going to kill me then and there. I could see the gun shaking as he gripped it more tightly.

He took a deep breath.

And he smiled.

"The games are over, Henry," he said, more calmly. Quite calmly, in fact. The transition itself was frightening, his transition upon entering from calm joviality to fury, and now so suddenly from terrible white-lipped fury back to the smiling, smiling villain. The rapidity of the transition gave meaning to what would otherwise have been puzzling, gave it meaning and definition. And made it more frightening. I had never before seen a real, living, actual schizophrenic.

"The games are over," he said. "The play is ended. The third-act curtain is ringing down."

"No one writes third acts anymore," I said. Not out of bravado, but in an effort to keep him talking, to jolly along his calm. His hands were no longer tight and shaking with fury, but they still held that obscene sawed-off shotgun, they still pointed it at me.

He smiled, shrugged. "I do apologize. I'm not a playwright, after all. Only a murderer."

"A murderer?"

"Meet it is, Henry. Write it down in your tables. That one may smile, and smile, and be a—murderer."

I asked, trying for a casual, matter-of-fact tone, "So you *did* kill Sarah?"

"Don't play games!" he hissed, on the verge of becoming Mr. Hyde again. "You know I killed her! You found Cissy!"

I had no choice but to try to talk him out of it. "Cissy didn't even know Sarah was dead—"

"Of course not! But *you* know! All Cissy knew was that we had played a little joke. But when she told you that, *you* knew what it meant." And suddenly he smiled again. His shoulders relaxed. I couldn't tell which of his personalities frightened me more. Which one was more likely to pull the trigger?

Which one had killed Sarah?

Which one had killed Billy Noel?

He pulled up a chair by the table and sat down, relaxed, the shotgun dangling from his fingers between his legs, more obscene than ever. "As soon as you talked to her," he said, "you must have known what it meant. Why else do you think I put you in touch with her? What's that?" He gestured easily with the gun, pointing behind me.

I half turned, afraid to take my eyes off the gun. The fear was making a child of me, like a child I clung to a wish—as long as I kept my eyes on that wicked gun, perhaps it wouldn't go off. I half turned, and out of the corner of my eye saw Cissy's note lying on the bed. I handed it to him.

He read it, smiling. "A dear child," he said. "A sweet innocent. A natural." He sighed. "We'll wait for her."

We waited.

I shivered. It was beginning to get cold. I started to get up.

He glanced at me. The shotgun in his hands moved with his eyes. Both pointed at me, eyes and gun. Two eyes and two shotgun barrels. And all four of them had about the same expression.

"I'm just going to get dressed," I said.

He stared at me.

I was afraid to move.

"Can I get dressed?" I asked.

He shook his head.

I sat down on the bed again.

We were quiet.

We looked at each other. We listened for the sound of Cissy's canoe. I tried to think what he was thinking, what he intended—

I suddenly remembered something he had said. "What did you mean?" I asked. "When you said that you put me in touch with Cissy? I found her myself."

He shook his head. "You never would have known she existed."

I didn't understand. He saw that. He enjoyed it. He laughed.

"*How* did you learn of her existence?" he asked.

"The pictures . . ."

"Who do you think sent them to you?" he asked.

And he laughed.

And I realized that there is nothing in the world so terrifying—nothing, not a shark cruising just under the waves, not an airliner out of control, not a masked gunman or a hidden sniper or aliens from another world—there is nothing in this world so terrifying as a madman, a laughing psychopath out of control.

"Who did you think?" he persisted, leaning forward in the chair now, chuckling. "Billy? Cissy? They must have told you they didn't. So who did you think? There wasn't anyone else."

"Why?" I asked.

"Why?" He stopped chuckling. He sat up straight. He gripped the gun tightly. Oh, Christ, we were off again. "Because I *wanted* you to know! Because I'm not done yet! You sneaking whining devious son of a bitch, did you think you were going to get off that easy? Did you think no one but Sarah was going to be punished? Did you think you were going to get out of this *alive?*" His voice rose and he followed it out of the chair. He stood over me, screaming, "No!"

And without transition the scream broke into a low chuckle and my blood froze and cracked into tiny little red icicles up and down my spine. "You are clever," he said. He shook his head and waggled his finger at me. "You were always clever. But I know what you're thinking. You want her to hear me in here, you want to make me lose my temper and scream so she'll hear me and have a chance to run away. Oh no, my friend. We shall be more clever than you. We shall sit here talking quietly while sweet Cissy buys her groceries and paddles back home. We shall wait here quietly as she walks up the trail from the lake. And then, as she opens the door and comes in, we shall kill her."

"Why?"

My throat was thick with fear: the word came rasping out.

"Why?" He laughed. Quietly. "So she'll tell no one else what she told you. Isn't that reason enough?" He lowered his eyelids, glowered at me from beneath them. "Reason enough," he repeated. He nodded. "Sufficient unto the day is the evil thereof. But of course there are more reasons," he whispered. "Many more."

I wasn't listening. I was thinking of how to get away. I tried to look around the room without moving my eyes from his face and from his gun. The door was over there beyond him. I'd never make it. I was naked, but that meant nothing—I'd run through Times Square and turn somersaults in Macy's window to get away—Macy's window. The window. There was a window to my left. I glanced at it. It was more than waist-high. I might be able to dive through it—but not before he could pull the trigger. And then what, anyhow? Naked and unarmed . . .

Unarmed.

The knife was on the table. The steel knife with which Cissy had slit and gutted the fish last night.

Turner sat down again. At the table. Oh, Christ, oh,

dear sweet Jesus Christ, I was helpless and this madman was going to kill me. . . .

"Turner," I said.

He looked at me.

I had to be careful. I had to handle him right. Surely he could be handled? He was, after all, my friend. Mad as a hatter, deadly as Himmler, but he *was* my friend. Surely I could *reach* him.

"Turner," I said softly, "I think I know why you sent me the pictures."

"Do you?"

"I think so." Softly, so softly. Carefully drop the bait into the pool. "Do you know why?"

"Me?" Just as softly. Amused. "Do I know why?"

"Do you?" Gently. Don't antagonize him, don't scare him away. Like walking a tightrope, carrying dynamite.

"Perhaps not." Smiling. "Do any of us ever know our real motivations? Tell me, dear boy. Tell me why."

Let the bait sink. Quietly, casually, "It's the old story, isn't it?"

"Is it? What old story?"

"The sick man, the lonely, frightened man who scrawls on the bathroom mirror, *Stop me before I kill again.* It's a call for help."

"A call for help?"

"Yes."

"From a sick man?"

"A tired man. To his friend."

"To *my* friend?"

"To me."

"To you? You? My friend?"

Did I have him? I sat there quietly, tensed on the edge of the bed, straining for the appearance of calm. I sat there quietly, a fisherman feeling the string, straining to feel if the trout was hooked. When is the time to reel in? Too soon, and you lose him. Too late, and he breaks the line. Did I have him?

"My friend?" he repeated softly. "My old friend? My dear friend, the friend who screws my wife?"

He was gone. I heard the line snap.

His voice rose. "My best friend, who comes home after nearly twenty years to throw my wife into bed? To fill her head with wicked stories and her with—"

He slammed his hand down on the table. I sat quietly in the reverberating room listening to his heaving breath. I had lost him forever. My only chance now, I thought, was to hear Cissy's canoe as she beached it. Then I would dive for the window. If I made it, perhaps I could get down to the water and we could shove off before he caught us. Then we might lose him in the fog.

It wasn't much of a chance. At close quarters he couldn't miss with a sawed-off shotgun.

And he was sitting not three feet from me.

He was sitting at the table, moving his head loosely from side to side.

All I had to do was get up and cross four feet of space and fling myself through the window and dive out.

All he had to do was squeeze the trigger.

It was getting very difficult to swallow my saliva.

"Shall I tell you my plan, old friend?" he asked. "My old and trusted friend. I trusted you with my wife, shall I trust you now with my plan? It will be a great comfort to you. For you are not going to die."

Jesus! Bastard! The old Gestapo trick, and I have to tell you it really works. He laughed at the expression in my eyes—the expression I couldn't control, of relief, of *gratitude!* The son of a bitch. The crazy murdering son of a bitch!

"You are not going to die. At least, *I* am not going to kill you. At least, not if you behave. If you try anything silly, of course there would then be no reason on earth why I shouldn't splatter your guts onto the walls of this lovely demimonde pied-à-terre in the wilderness, *n'est-ce pas?*

"But . . . if you're a very good little boy, if you listen to Papa, *if* you are an obedient little coward, why then you shall live."

I tried to use his sadism to get myself angry. I tried to concentrate on his trying to torture me so that I could hate, so that the hate and the anger might take over and drive the numbing fear from my mind.

"What we shall do, sweet Henry, is sit here quietly waiting for our Cissy to come home with the breakfast goodies. Softly softly catchee monkey. We shall sit here quietly talking of many things, of shoes and ships and sealing wax . . . and whether pigs have wings, of the comradely manner in which you stole my Sarah's love, perverted her nature, defiled her soul—and finally we shall hear the soft splish-splashing of little Cissy's paddle in the water, the gentle footfall of her little feet as she climbs the trail to our cabin by the shore, we shall hear the click of the door latch opening, the creak of the door-jamb as the door itself opens, the sudden splash of color as her lithe form fills the doorway—by the way, what is she wearing this morning? Her blue jeans, the gray sweat shirt?"

I didn't answer. He glanced around the cabin. "No," he said, "there's her sweat shirt. She wouldn't go out topless for groceries, would she? Not even Cissy would do that. Maybe in Miami, but surely not in upstate New York. What's her other lake outfit? Oh yes, the lumberjack shirt. She must be wearing that. The one with the glorious colors, reds and greens and yellows all checkerboarded together. Such a lovely shirt. Such a lovely girl. Dear Cissy.

"So here shall we sit, the revenge-crazed murderer and the sniveling predator of married women, the silent coward and the silent killer, here shall we two sit and wait as she beaches the canoe, climbs the trail laden with groceries, kicks open the door, and fills its opening with her blue jeans and glorious gallimaufric shirt signaling the moment—

"And then boom!"

He raised the shotgun.

"As she steps through that door I shall kill her."

He paused.

"And that will be the end," he said, "of the only evidence linking me to Sarah's death. And you will sit here quietly and watch it happen."

He shrugged.

"Oh, you could call out, of course. You could warn her. But if you do, you will die." He held up the shotgun. "Two triggers, you see. Two charges. Two shells. If you make one sound I'll blast your face open and then chase her down and dispatch her. Can you imagine what it must feel like to catch the blast of a sawed-off shotgun in the face? Or perhaps the intestines, the guts, that might be even better. Especially as you stand naked, with your proud sex hanging limp as a target beacon."

My stomach muscles contracted instinctively in fear, each molecule trying to draw the others around it for comfort and protection. He saw it, he didn't miss a thing. He laughed.

"But if you are the self-seeking coward I am sure you are, you will simply sit quietly and watch it happen. After that, I shall leave you."

He was enjoying my mystification as much as my fear. "Oh yes, I shall leave. I shall walk down to the water, get into my canoe, and push off from shore. I shall remove the second charge from this weapon and shall throw said charge out into the lake. I shall turn and throw the weapon to you as you stand helplessly onshore, splattered by her blood. And I shall then disappear into the soft morning fog.

"And you shall decide, my old and trusted friend, *you* shall decide how best to notify the police. And what to tell them."

It was a sort of schizophrenia that I was feeling myself, a physical sort of double existence. From the neck down I was frightened, physically frightened. My body down there was beyond control, separate. My toes were cold, my knees knocked together, my guts trembled on the brink of involuntary defecation, the skin over my stomach crawled, the hairs on my arms stood up, there were goose pimples running wild up my spine. But above the neck I was calm, fascinated. There was a sense of *déjà vu* that was comforting. This was Turner, my old friend. He was talking calmly, rationally, and if the words themselves were crazy—why, that seemed to penetrate only to the visceral senses below my neck. Up here in my conscious mind the weather was fine, ceiling and visibility unlimited, with only mild clear-air turbulence. . . .

"I have some suggestions, of course," he said, waving the shotgun casually, as if it were a swagger stick or some amusing doohickey he had picked up passing through India. "You may take them for what they're worth. For instance, you might simply care to leave. Take the other canoe, you know, and paddle off into the fog. Catch the next bus back to Watkins Glen, et cetera, and so forth higgledy-piddledy back to your own little home in New

York. And there huddle safely. Secure in your premises.

"As I was secure in my home. With my wife. As I *thought* I was secure. Until you trampled down my walls and fornicated with my wife. Eh? What do you say?"

He seemed so calm I thought for a moment I really could talk to him, reason with him. "Turner," I said, "I don't deny I loved Sarah. I always loved her. Don't you remember? We *both* loved her. And then she chose you."

"Me."

"Yes—"

"And settled down with me to live happily ever after. And so we did. As man and wife. And then came the serpent in the garden!" he exploded again. "The wolf in the manger! The fly in the ointment—" He began to laugh. I couldn't stand it. He was crazy. "Like a Noël Coward song, isn't it?" he laughed. "I thought it was a fly in the ointment," he chanted in a singsong voice, "a nigger in the woodpile, but it was you, you, you. . . ."

I had broken out into a spontaneous sweat when he exploded this time, and now I was cold. I wished I had at least my pants on. He suddenly broke off singing.

"Quiet! What was that?"

We both sat there, leaning slightly forward, listening. There was a soft slap-slap of water on the shore. A canoe being beached? Or just the wind?

Oh, please God, I prayed, not yet. Please not yet. I didn't have a plan yet. I hadn't thought of anything to do. What *could* I do? I couldn't let her walk in and be murdered. I couldn't let him shoot *me*. Please God, more time, give me more time—

He stood up, tiptoed to the window, and looked out.

"Can't see a damned thing in this fog," he muttered.

His back was to me.

The knife was on the table.

I stood up.
The bed creaked.
He turned around.
He smiled.
The shotgun in his hand was pointing straight at my belly.
I felt sick.
I was going to vomit.
He took two steps toward me. Stood face to face with me, smiling. Moved the gun toward me. Touched its gaping tip against my stomach. Cold. Dropped the tip just a bit. Touched it to my penis.
I closed my eyes.
He laughed.
He pushed with the gun and I stumbled back and fell down on the bed. My legs had no strength. I couldn't have leaped on him and wrestled the gun from him, if the lives of all humanity depended on it. I could no more do that than fly.

Oh, God, it's not *really* going to happen?

He nodded at the window. "It's not her," he said. "Only the wind. The passing wind. Well, well, we must wait, mustn't we? What were we talking about?"

The sudden return to normalcy, the reprieve, was the most welcome relief I have ever experienced—and at the same time it was the most debilitating aspect of the whole scene. My feet and hands were trembling. I couldn't cope with another round of horror.

"What *were* we talking about?" he asked. "Oh yes, of course, I remember. You were asking my advice. Well, you could, as I say, simply leave and go home and hope for the best. Hope that no one will ever connect you with the tragically murdered *poule* on the shores of far-off Lake Charles. It should be possible. I see no difficulty. In this fog you should have no problem leaving without being seen. I anticipate no such difficulty myself. Unless, of course, you made the terribly silly mistake of being seen when you arrived?"

"You must have been seen, too."

He shook his head.

"You couldn't have found us without talking to the manager."

He smiled. "Dear boy," he said, "this cabin is nothing new to me. This is *our* cabin. Oh yes," he smiled happily, seeing something in my face I couldn't control. "Cissy's and mine. We've been here before." He laughed suddenly. "What a rage is on your face! Could it possibly be —no, it couldn't! Not possibly! You couldn't have *fallen* for my little whore?" He clapped his hands in delight, the shotgun swinging wildly. "But how delicious! More than I could *possibly* have hoped for! Perhaps there really is a God in heaven? Will *you* now feel the pangs of despised love, the torturous stinging nettles of jealousy? Will wonders never cease?"

He looked out the window again. Minutes ticked by in silence. "Where *is* the bitch?" he asked.

He turned and looked at me, frowned, seemed surprised to see me here. "What were we talking about? My mind seems to wander so these days. And you're no help," he said severely, "with your scarcely contained jealousy. Well, well. You could go home, as I say. And hope that the manager here has forgotten you. Unless, of course, you were so incredibly careless as to register with your own name. But no, that's not fair of me, you weren't anticipating Cissy's demise, were you? You didn't know I was coming."

"How did you know where she was?"

"The same way you knew. I visited her little place in Miami and found the note in the typewriter."

I told him what I had done there, how I'd removed her note. I told him about the message I'd left in its place.

He laughed. "Too funny, old son. But of course I had already been there. I went there first, before I found Billy."

"The old woman said no one had been there looking for Cissy."

"She wasn't home at the time. It was the old man who let me in."

I had him. "Then he knows you were looking for her. If you kill her, he'll testify—"

"To nothing. I gave him a false name. Timothy O'Leary, theatrical agent." He smiled. "Don't be upset. You tried. So you win some and you lose some."

"He'll identify you—"

"He'll identify no one." He sighed. "The poor old dear is blind, you see. Syphilis, probably. Southern aristocracy. Terribly decadent." He was enjoying himself, the son of a bitch. "So what else have we?" He held up his hands. "Gloves, my dear. Ergo no fingerprints on the gun, or anywhere in this cabin or on my 'borrowed' canoe. Whereas you, I imagine, must have left the odd fingerprint on various items around and about the cabin. Not to mention, I'm sure, the dozens of fingerprints left on every available inch of poor Cissy's body. Will you be able to wipe them all off? Will you work your way inch by inch through the cabin, wiping and polishing every surface, while Cissy's bloody dead body lies grotesquely sprawled on the floor, gathering flies? Will you, indeed? I hope so, the spectacle is titillating. But I think not. No, I rather think that your only recourse is to stick to your story."

"What story?" I shouldn't be talking to him, I desperately needed time to think. But I couldn't help it. Like a fly caught in the web, and fascinated by the spider. By its sheer ugliness and terror.

"Your only possible story. That Turner killed his wife—despite your own account of the events which proves that impossible. Oh yes, you then tell them Cissy's strange story. But Cissy is dead. Ergo, no corroboration. How is she dead? Murdered most cruelly while alone with you here. And who else? Why, Billy Noel. Murdered most cruelly while you were in Miami. Coincidence? Does anyone really believe in coincidence? I'm afraid not. Oh dear. Oh dear, dear."

"You have no alibi for today—"

"Well, of course not. I can't possibly have anyone who has seen me in, say, Montauk today—since I'm not there. I am here, am I not? *But* several weeks ago I talked by phone to an ancient lady who runs a summer cottage community out there. She wants to retire, get out of the business, sell it all. I told her I'd like to see it, with an eye toward taking it over. She lives out the winters in Boston, but she told me where the keys are hidden and said I might visit there at my leisure. I called her yesterday and asked if I might go there tomorrow—today, you see. Actually, I took the liberty of going there last week. So nobody has actually *seen* me there today, but it's deserted at this time of year, and no one could be expected to. And if the police check, they'll find my fingerprints all over everything out there. So it's not an airtight alibi, but quite a reasonable one.

"What else? Oh yes. Blood."

Do you remember Olivier as Richard the Third? The eyes? The smiling face—and those hooded evil eyes?

"The blood," he repeated. "We must take care of the blood. Let's run through the blocking, shall we? When we hear her beach the canoe, you will take up position there, stage right." He gestured toward the door. "We really should have chalk or tape to mark the floor, but since it's only just the one scene perhaps you'll be good enough to remember your moves?"

He stood up and walked to the door. Opened it—it opened inward—and stationed himself just beyond its radius of opening. "Here," he said. "You will stand exactly here. Understood?"

He now moved behind the open door. "I will stand unobtrusively here." He stood there, then stepped quickly one pace to his left, to the opening of the door, leaned and extended his arm, and pointed the shotgun around the door into the open doorway. "Kaboom," he said. "Point-blank range. Impossible to miss. Perfect. What were we talking about?"

He stared at me.

Hypnotized by his evil, I answered. "The blood," I said.

His face was calm, his eyes were wild. *La Belle Dame sans Merci.* "The blood," he repeated. "The blood will splatter, fly, explode all over. You will be standing three feet away. You will be drenched in her blood. But—staged perfectly, I shall be behind the door, shielded, pristinely pure, and so I shall remain. And you? Will you wash away her blood? Will you wash away every drop before the police come?"

He laughed. "I wish you more luck than Lady Macbeth."

His laugh stopped, choked off abruptly. His eyes were hard, shining.

"So," he said in a new tone of voice. "The stage is set. The curtain is ready to go up. Now we sit. And wait."

And wait.

Outside, the sun was surely rising, but without effect. The fog hung heavy on the ground, draped from the trees that stood nearly invisible in the frame of the window. Condensation dripped from the wooden eaves to the ground outside, the only sound, soft, quiet, plop-plop, plop . . . plop.

Inside, there were only two objects in focus; everything else was blurred and misty. There was, first, the shotgun held limply in Turner's hand. And then, behind him, on the table, the fish knife. Long and thin, tapering to a point.

I tried not to look at it. If he saw me looking at it, if he noticed it, all he had to do was pick it up and put it in a drawer or throw it out the window. And I would be lost. For it was the only chance I could see.

It wasn't much of a chance. Not much, against the double-barreled sawed-off shotgun.

Seconds.

Minutes.

Plop-plop, plop . . . plop.

We strained for the first sound of Cissy.

I couldn't stand the silence. I couldn't keep my eyes off the knife. Turner's eyes swiveled from the door to me, back to the closed door. I glanced at the knife—he almost saw me! Oh, God . . .

"Turner."

"What?"

"Why?"

He looked at me. "Why?" He seemed puzzled.

"Why did you do it?"

"Do what?"

"Kill Sarah!" Good God, *do what?* "Why on earth did you kill her?"

His eyes streamed hate at me. "You ask me that?" He

was hissing, his lips tight, white with sudden fury. "*You* ask me that?"

I didn't believe that he had killed only for jealousy, for love.

Can you kill someone you love?

His eyes shone hate, pure white hate.

Surely he hadn't killed Sarah because of me?

"Look, Turner," I pleaded, "listen—"

"Look," he mimicked cruelly, "listen. Yes, that is exactly what I did. I looked, and was quiet. I listened, and waited. I looked and I saw! I listened and I heard!"

"I didn't love your wife!"

"Liar!"

Oh, Christ. What could I say? "No, listen." I held up my hands, pleading. "Yes, I *did* love her. But not that way!"

"*Which way*, then, fornicator?"

"I loved her like a friend—" I broke off. I couldn't lie to those eyes, not for my life. The hate in those eyes was no longer pure. It was still there, it shone there brightly, but there now was something else with it. There was pain. There was suffering. Oh, God, why had I done it? Why had I gone to bed with her? I had wanted to be her friend, his friend, to each of them a friend.

"I loved her," I said, trying to explain to him, trying to explain to myself, trying to understand it myself, "I did love her when I left you. Years ago. I came back when I was over it, when I accepted you, accepted your marriage—"

"Accepted it. And violated it!"

How had he known? Does the husband always, eventually, know? Or had he seen the fornication in my eyes as I had seen the murder in his? Had I preened myself on his cuckoldry? Oh, Christ . . .

"Never mind," he said wearily, lowering his eyes, tired suddenly of the whole discussion. "Never mind, it doesn't signify."

I wanted to explain.

I couldn't.

I was guilty, after all. And however much you talk, you cannot explain away guilt.

"You knew I killed her, right from the start, didn't you?" he asked. I nodded. "But you didn't know how, did you?" He was calm again. "I could have stopped right there, you know. I was home scot-free, the murder would never have been solved."

"But you didn't. You sent me the pictures."

"Of course. I didn't want to kill Sarah. Why would I want to do that? I loved Sarah. I killed her because she was no longer mine, no longer Sarah my wife. You had taken her from me, changed her, turned her into something else. So if she had to die because you had taken her from me, certainly it didn't make sense to allow you to live. Am I right? Does that sound nonsensical to you? Does it sound illogical? Does it sound crazy?"

I didn't know how to answer him. I didn't want to start him off again. I thought if I could keep him calm until Cissy came, surely he wouldn't shoot her in cold blood. Surely he had to work himself up into a tantrum? So I nodded.

"Yes," he said. "It stands to reason. But how to kill you? After your accusations, any means of death—no matter how seemingly accidental—would surely throw suspicion on me. It was a difficult problem."

I nodded appreciatively.

"You look silly naked," he said. "As I say, as you can appreciate, it was a difficult problem. But I worked it out. And began to maneuver. Sent you the photos. You thought you were so clever, but I anticipated your every thought. I had your every reaction, your every move, planned out in advance. And you did exactly as I planned. When you went to Miami, I followed and killed poor Billy. And now I have you here for the final act. And there is nothing you can do. I've worked it all out, you see.

"If you insist on bravado, I'll kill you here and now. And then kill Cissy. Murder and suicide will be the obvious explanation. You killed Sarah out of jealousy, you killed Cissy for the same reason. The photos, you see. On the other hand, if you stand there quietly while Cissy dies, you will certainly live out your days in jail with her blood on your hands. With her blood splattered all over your body, in fact. I think that would be more satisfactory, don't you? Give you time to think, don't you see? Time to regret, as it were. Yes, I think that would be better all around."

"It won't work," I said, trying to stay calm as a sudden idea hit me, saving me, saving our lives. "It won't work, you can't do it."

"Why not? Oh, I see! You've finally thought of it, have you? The old gray cells finally working?"

"The gun," I said, becoming excited despite myself. "Your sawed-off shotgun—"

"Yes, the gun!" He was beginning to get excited. "What of it?"

"You didn't buy that gun—"

"I bought it in Miami, on the day you were there. The store sells a dozen a day—no license required in Florida, you see. He'll never remember me, and if they can trace the sale they'll find it was bought on the one day that you were in town."

"But you bought a shotgun! Not a *sawed-off* shotgun. Nobody sells sawed-off shotguns, they're illegal!"

"Yes, you're beginning to think! Out with it, then!"

"You didn't sit out in Central Park cutting it down, did you?"

"No, of course not!"

"Of course not! You had to be somewhere private, alone. So somewhere there are metal filings—"

"Yes!" he shouted. "Where?"

I was stunned. I fell back, exhausted. I thought he hadn't thought of that. I thought—

"You thought," he said, "that somewhere in my house would be telltale metal filings and shavings. Poor fool. Outsmarted at every turn. Yes, somewhere there are such shavings. Can you guess where?"

Total defeat.

"In your apartment," he said, smiling softly. "Those old city places are so easy to enter. Without leaving a trace, I'm sure. Just a celluloid card in the lock. My Visa card, actually. I spent yesterday afternoon there, sawing off the gun. The shavings, the powder, will have settled inextricably into the floorboard cracks. Final and irrefutable evidence."

He had thought of everything, hadn't he? But it wasn't going to come to that, so it didn't matter. I wasn't going to let him kill Cissy. It was funny, but all this talk was calming me down; not him, but *me*. I think I was beginning to accept the situation. All right. He was mad, and he had a gun. All right. What then? There was the knife on the table. Somehow that knife had to be my salvation.

"Quiet!" he whispered, and my guts leaped up into my throat again.

We listened.

There was a bird out there.

There was the lap of the tiny waves.

A breeze, and the rustle of leaves.

The bird left, the flutter of its wings soon lost in the fog.

The breeze died. The waves settled down.

It was quiet again.

There was no sound and no sight beyond this cabin, there was only the silent fog and a slowly burgeoning wave of despair that rose out of it and settled over me like a heavy woolen blanket. It was all such a waste.

"Such a waste," I said.

"Don't talk," he said. "We'd better be quiet now. She has to get back soon. Anyway, there's nothing left to be said."

"There is!" I was angry and sad at the same time. And terribly frightened, of course, but the fear was settling in as a permanent part of me, one I didn't have to pay constant attention to. "There's a lot to be said. You must know how mistaken you are. I want you to understand you did it all for nothing. Sarah loved you."

"Until you stole her."

"I didn't steal her! Don't you remember Sarah? Don't you remember what she was like? She never changed. Yes, we went to bed—and so what? That didn't mean anything to her. She *loved* you, don't you understand? She loved only *you*, right up to the moment you slashed her throat!"

"Shut up!"

"I won't shut up! You stupid selfish bastard, it was *you* she wanted, not me! She only wanted me to help her get you back—"

"Back? Get me back? I never left her—"

"Oh yes you did! You had retreated into that crazy mind of yours—and she was locked out. She was afraid she was losing you, day by day. And she was afraid *of* you—"

"Never! Never! She was never afraid of me, she loved me, she trusted me—" He broke off, confused. "Until you came back."

I shook my head. "She asked me to help. She told me she was afraid—"

"You lie! What had she to be afraid of? She'd never say that! She knew I wouldn't harm a hair of her head!"

"You slit her throat! You killed her!"

The words hung in the air like a bomb burst. He stared at me, the tears bulged in his eyes, he dropped his head into his hands.

"I loved her," he said. "Right from the beginning I loved her. You never did. Never. I was the one who always loved her. . . ."

His head was buried in his hands. His eyes were closed. The fish knife glistened on the table. I pressed my palms down on the mattress, elbows stiff, trying to hold the bed still—trying to keep it from squeaking as I slowly lifted my weight from it. Carefully, I inched my weight forward onto the balls of my feet.

"I knew it meant nothing when she married me, but when you went away I thought I had won. For a few years it was wonderful. Then she began to think about you. I could see it, I knew what went on in her mind, I could see her beginning to think about you again. She began to write to you—"

I had my weight on my feet now. I began to ease forward off the bed, releasing the pressure on the mattress with my hands slowly, letting it rise quietly—and it squeaked.

"She never wrote," I said loudly to cover the noise.

"She never once wrote to me. When we met, it was by accident."

He didn't look up. He didn't hear me, he didn't hear the mattress. "I didn't blame her," he said. "You know Sarah. She couldn't help it, she was a victim. It was your fault. Oh yes, my friend, your fault. My *friend.* I wouldn't even have minded, if you had loved her. I wouldn't have minded. All I wanted was for her own good. But I knew you. You wanted her money, you wanted the real estate—"

I was off the bed now. I was standing three feet from him. And just behind him was the knife. The shotgun hung loosely in his hands, and his hands covered his face. I could grab the gun, or the knife, with two steps. I slid my right foot across the floor, slowly. It mustn't creak with my weight. . . .

"You wanted the real estate business that I had built up, I knew that. I had built it from nothing, from a hole in the wall. But her father had put it in her name. He never trusted me. You would have taken her from me and taken the business with her, you couldn't make a living writing your stupid plays and so you came back to her and made love to her, seduced her from me, desecrated and destroyed her—"

I was halfway to him. My weight was now on my right foot. I brought my left foot slowly across the floor. I could almost reach him now. One more step.

"Ahoy!"

His head snapped up.

"Ahoy the cabin!" came Cissy's gay shout from the lake.

He blinked. At me.

"Are you awake yet, you lazy pig?" she called.

I tensed to spring.

The shotgun came up. His fingers were sliding loose, scrabbling for the trigger.

I leaped at him, hands outflung—

His gloved fingers couldn't find the trigger.

I was on him. He stumbled backward against the table—

My fingers missed the gun, found his throat, reached for his eyes—

He lifted the gun in both hands and swung it like a club. He caught me across the side of the head with the short metal barrel.

I fell across the table. Slid off it. Fell heavily to the floor. Lay there, stunned. He stretched out the gun toward me, pointed it into my face—

In the sudden silence the firing pin clicked back as he slowly squeezed the trigger.

In the long, slow silence her bare footsteps came slap-slap up the path toward the door.

His finger on the trigger froze. He listened to Cissy coming closer.

Without relaxing his trigger finger he motioned with the gun. His finger stayed taut. The firing pin hung back, ready to snap forward with the slightest change in pressure. He motioned me to get up and take my place inside the door.

I shifted my weight and felt a pain in the buttock. I had fallen on something sharp. I felt under me as I rose to my knees. It was the knife.

His eyes were on me. My eyes locked into his. His finger was tight on the trigger. My fingers closed around the knife, held it under my thigh as I slowly got to my feet.

He didn't notice.

He gestured me to the door. I moved around him, turning as I went so the knife stayed hidden, pressed against the back of my thigh.

Her footsteps came up to the door.

Stopped.

Silence.

A soft rustling outside. The fog swallowed all noise.

We waited.

When she opened the door he would have to take his beady eyes off me. He would have to shift his attention to her, would have to swing the gun around, aim it—

And I would throw the knife. It was our only chance. One throw.

I held the knife tightly against my thigh. It was wet, sticky. It must have cut me when I fell on it. I tried to shift my fingers around on the handle without moving so that he wouldn't notice— I almost dropped it! Christ, forget it, this would have to do.

The door creaked, began to open.

He didn't shift his gaze, keeping me riveted.

The door swung wide. Cissy's voice chirped loudly, "Ta-raa!"

There was the flash of color in the doorway—the red and green and yellow checkered lumberjack shirt, the blue jeans—

And Turner simply moved the gun in a quick circle away from me and around the edge of the door and pulled the trigger.

Blam!

The explosion rocked the cabin, stunned me, deafened me. The lumberjack shirt and blue jeans disappeared in a white and black cloud, exploded into dust.

I threw the knife.

Too late, I was already screaming. Too late.

It hit him in the head—sideways. Flat. Useless. It only

startled him so that he banged against the door, slamming it closed against the jamb. He blinked and turned the gun back toward me.

I was paralyzed.

The door hit hard against the jamb and bounced back, swinging wide.

I didn't want to see what was there as it swung open. Horrified, I looked.

Cissy stood there.

Naked.

Stunned.

Her right hand still held stiffly straight out to the side, still holding the tattered, torn remnants of her lumberjack shirt and jeans into which Turner had fired.

In one long second that stretched off into the distant past I realized what had happened. She had come up to the cabin, paused outside, stripped off her clothes as a surprise, and swung the door open to stand there like the Statue of Liberty. And Turner had quickly turned and fired into her outstretched dangling clothes.

Blood now welled out of her hand and arm. She was too shocked to scream, to move.

"Run!" I shouted. "He wants to kill you! Run!"

Turner turned and saw her. He lifted the gun to her face.

Pulled the trigger.

Click.

Again.

Click.

Frozen in horror, all of us.

"Run!" I screamed.

Turner must have pulled both triggers in that first shot. The gun was not loaded. We both realized it at the same time. "Run!" I screamed again and leaped at him. He raised the gun again as a club, but I was ready this time. I grabbed it with both hands. Cissy disappeared from the doorway. Turner kicked me in the balls.

I dropped like a sack. The pain started down there and just spread through me, enveloped me. I couldn't move, couldn't breathe. I lay on the floor as Turner pulled two shells out of his pocket, broke open the shotgun, and began to stuff them in.

I didn't want to die. But I just couldn't move. "Run," I tried to call to vanished Cissy, but nothing came out. A wave of nausea came up instead.

Turner snapped the gun shut. Glanced at me. Decided I would wait, I wasn't going anywhere. He ran to the door.

Nothing there now but fog.

He stepped out and disappeared into the fog.

The knife lay just inside the door.

I took a breath. The air came into my lungs this time, and with it came life. Just barely. But enough. I crawled toward the knife. The movement helped. I could feel my toes again.

The cabin was so quiet. The fog swirled in the empty doorway. Cissy's mangled clothes lay there, splattered with a few drops of blood. I got up on my knees, then on my feet—

Turner swirled into the doorway with the fog. He wasn't talking now. He simply stood there and raised the gun and held it out in both hands, pointing it at me.

The knife was still two feet away. Infinitely far away. Too goddamn infinitely far away. I spun around away from him, slipped, took two quick steps, and dove through the open window.

Behind me the gun exploded. I landed hard on the dirt and my breath went again. I rolled and kept rolling. I knew I couldn't get to my feet again. So I rolled and rolled and the nausea came up again and enveloped me and I didn't care, I just rolled and rolled until the yellow nausea enveloped me inside and the white fog enveloped me outside and finally I was alone with them, just me and the nausea and the white white fog.

I retched.

I rested.

I crawled now, slowly, painfully, away from the nausea and deeper into the fog.

It was quiet, and I was folded into the fog. I lay there and waited, listening.

I heard footsteps.

I lay quietly. Tried to breathe quietly.

The footsteps came closer, closer, louder, then fainter. I grew dizzy trying to listen. I put my head down in the cool dirt and just breathed.

The footsteps faded away.

It was quiet.

"Cissy!"

His sudden shout startled me.

"Cissy!"

No answer.

I had to find her. I had to find her before he did. If we could get down to the lake unseen, if we could push off in the canoe, even if he heard us and came after us we'd have a good chance in the fog.

I even thought for a moment of forgetting Cissy, just getting down to the lake and pushing off in the canoe. To get help, I told myself.

I told myself to shut up. I wasn't going without Cissy. But I had to find her first. Before he did.

"Cissy!" he called again in a strained holler, a guttural shout. "Cissy, listen to me!"

Silence. I listened, as he must be doing, for the sound of running, of footsteps.

Nothing. She was hiding in the fog. Smart girl. Stay hidden. But how am I going to find you?

"Cissy Massenick, please hear me!" he was calling in that guttural voice. "Your life depends on this. I am Lieutenant Paul Douglass of the Suffolk County Police Department—"

What?

"—and your life is in danger, Cissy. Henry Grace is a murderer. I followed him here as he followed you. He is wanted by the police for the murder of Mrs. Sarah Turner. That silly trick you played on him with Turner triggered it off; he went back that same night and really killed her! Now he wants to kill you! He's a psychopath, Cissy! That stupid joke of yours threw his mind off balance—"

How could he expect her to believe that? She had seen him, she had seen him try to kill her—or had she? She had opened the door and the shotgun had exploded in her face. Then when he shoved the shotgun into her eyes and pulled the trigger and it clicked empty, would she have been able to see anything except the yawning open twin barrels six inches from her nose? Could she have focused on anything else? Had she recognized him in that instant? And then she had run off into the fog. Had she seen him at all?

"It's not true, Cissy!" I shouted. "It's Turner, he's trying to trick you! He killed Sarah!"

No answer from Cissy, but from the direction of the cabin came footsteps. Oh, Christ, if I called to her he could follow my voice!

The footsteps came closer, half a dozen of them, then

stopped. He hadn't quite found me. He was listening again.

Silence. I held my breath.

"Cissy!" he called. "He's trying to trick you. Stay away from him, he wants to kill you! Your only chance is to come back to the cabin."

What could I do? If she believed him, if she went back to the cabin, he'd kill her and leave me here as he planned. If I tried to reason with her, he'd find me. Then with me dead, she'd be helpless.

"Cissy, that's Turner!" I shouted. "He killed Sarah, believe me!" Just a short shout, maybe he couldn't zero in on it—

No. In the silence that followed I heard his soft footsteps on the damp leaves. Coming closer. Two, three, four steps. Then silence. He was waiting.

He was too close now for me to call again. Did she believe me? Or him? If she stayed hidden from both of us it was stalemate . . . but he would win a stalemate. Night would come, and even now it was cold and damp. We were both naked, we were hurt, we would die of exposure and cold alone and naked in the wet forest.

I moved stealthily away. A twig cracked, the leaves rustled, I tripped and fell. I lay without moving. Silence. I crawled.

"Cissy," he called again. "For God's sake come back to the cabin. Listen to me! He killed Billy Noel. He killed Sarah Turner. You can't trust him. He looks sane, but he's a psychopath. Come back, Cissy."

The same argument he had used on the *pizzella*. It had worked with her. She'd believed him. Cissy would, too. Christ, I almost believed it myself! Bleeding, naked, alone and cold and frightened in the forest, she must feel an overwhelming urge to believe that someone who could help was here. Daddy, help! Save me! She couldn't hold out against that. I had to do something before she gave in. I had to find her, talk to her face to face, convince her—

How could I find her? He was waiting for me to call to her . . . stalking me . . .

I moved away as quietly as I could. She had to be out here somewhere. She would probably head for the lake. But where was the lake? I couldn't see more than a few feet away. I had lost any sense of direction. I had no idea where she was, or where I was. I only knew that Turner was not far away.

"Cissy," he called, "he's armed! He has a gun—"

If only I had!

"—he tried to shoot you in the cabin! Don't let him near you! Come back to the cabin, where I can protect you. You'll be safe, I promise you. This nightmare will be over!"

I moved quietly away from his voice. After a dozen steps without his following me I began to whisper. "Cissy? It's me. Cissy?"

It was no use. I was lost, blind. She was terrified. She was hiding and I'd never find her. We would die out here—

No!

No, by God, by all the gods, I would not let him get away with it! He had killed Sarah and made me the fall guy, but he wasn't going to get away with it! He *wasn't* going to kill Cissy, he wasn't going to leave me here to take the blame, he wasn't going to go off and live happily ever after! He wasn't! I would stop him!

Then I stopped raving and began to think.

How? How would I stop him?

He was the hunter, I was the prey. How could I turn

the tables? I was unarmed. If only I had that fish knife—what could I do with a knife against the gun? I could surprise him—yes, that was it. Surprise. If I could circle behind him, leap on him, knock the gun away—but how?

He was quiet now. Listening. For Cissy or for me. The hunter stalking the deer.

No.

The hunter stalking the tiger, by God.

And sometimes the tiger wins.

I had a plan. It was sudden, it was simple, it was going to be all or nothing, win or lose, and then it would be over. One way or the other.

I moved silently through the forest. Not stumbling now, not crawling, not tripping and falling and thrashing and crashing about with fear. Silently now, with stealth, with cunning. With a plan. The tiger, not the helpless deer.

It made all the difference in the world.

I moved slowly, inspecting each tree. I could see only a few feet in the fog, and so went from tree to tree until I found a good one. Old and thick, with a heavy limb I could barely reach by jumping.

I had to be sure I could reach it. One chance was all I'd get. I jumped up, grabbed the heavy limb with both hands, chinned myself to be sure I still had the strength. I did. The strength of desperation. Nothing is stronger.

I dropped back lightly to the ground.

Okay.

Now.

Sudden terror again—no! Stifle it, choke it down. If I lose—don't think of it. Don't think at all. Act.

Now.

"Cissy!" I called loudly. "Don't go to him! Hide, darling, hide!"

Pause for breath.

Silence.

Footsteps. Coming toward me, toward my voice. Hard to gauge how far away in this fog. *Must* gauge. Must be accurate. Listen. Far away. Too far away. But coming closer.

"Just stay hidden, Cissy! I swear it'll be all right—just don't move. He's not a policeman, it's Turner, he wants to kill you. It was—"

Close now.

A movement in the fog! Oh, Christ, too close!

I reached up, jumped, grabbed the branch. Chinned myself as before, but now didn't drop back to the ground. I swung my legs up to wrap them around the limb.

Missed!

Legs dropped heavily, swung around wildly. Must get them up! Must disappear up there before he finds me! Swing them up—

I wrapped one ankle around the limb, anchored it there, swung up the other, caught the limb. Thank God. Shifted around now, got on top of the limb. Safe.

Quiet.

Wait.

Footsteps. Coming closer.

They stop.

Will he come?

Movement, there, below. The fog moves, a sapling bends—

He steps through.

Foreshortened from this unnatural angle, swirled about with the clinging fog, nothing more than a vague black break in the fog, unrecognizable. But wearing a coat. Not naked. Not Cissy. Moving quietly, but not frightened.

Slow, stalking, one step at a time, stalking, listening, searching.

And too far away.

If he turns away he'll be lost again in the fog.

He nearly does. Takes one step to the right and half disappears into the fog.

He stops.

Takes one step back. Back into view. Three more steps, please! Three more steps and don't look up!

A patch of fog moves in on an unfelt breeze and blots him out.

Christ, where is he? He could pass right under me now and I'd never see him.

The fog parts for a moment, twists, and then hides him again.

But I have seen him for that one moment.

He has moved diagonally.

Standing now to my left. His back to me. Another step and he'll be *past* me.

Hidden now in the fog.

I cannot leap into that viscous fog.

Please, *please*, part this fog! Blow it away—

For one quick second it shifts, I catch a glimpse of his legs. His back is still enveloped in the mist. His legs are there—they're taking a step away from me—

I lift myself quickly on the tree limb, lift to a crouch. Too far away, but it must be now. I spring—

Through the air.

Not flying. Falling.

Heavily.

Stretch out—

And hit him!

Barely seeing him, my outstretched arms strike him across the head and neck, breaking my fall. Barely. I slam into the dirt and leaves, he's knocked sprawling. A sharp and terrible pain in my right ankle, a more terrifying numbness in the right knee—

He moves. Lifts himself to his knees.

All my weight on my left foot, I lunge and fall on him. Ignore the pain in my right leg. Hands around his neck. Twist him around, choke him—

The *pizzella!*

My God, it's the *pizzella!*

Not Turner. . . .

I collapse, fall to the ground beside her.

"What," I gasp, "how—?"

She can't answer, she rubs her throat.

"Does it really matter?" Turner asks.

I turn.

There he is. Shotgun raised. Aimed at us.

I'd had one chance, all or nothing.

Nothing.

"I've been . . ." the *pizzella* begins. She clears her throat, tries again. "I've been looking for you," she says to Turner.

"I'm sure it's an interesting story," he says. "Some other time."

She gets to her feet slowly, in pain. Stretches out one arm, grimaces. "That'll be black and blue tomorrow," she says.

"I'm afraid not," Turner says.

She looks down at me. I'm lying in the dirt and leaves, naked, bloody, scratched and torn and streaked with grass and dirt. And the fog is probably blurring the penetrating blue of my eyes. "A pretty sight," she says. "What games have you been playing?"

Far to my right, another sound. Another face pokes through the fog. Cissy. Alone and frightened, hearing the voices. Couldn't resist coming to see what was happening. Damned fool.

"Come in, my dear," Turner says. "Take one little step backward and I fire."

What can she do? She moves out of the fog and stands by us.

Her arm is smeared with blood, but not too much, not flowing rivers. It doesn't hide her beauty. I can't think of much that could. She stands in the glimmering wisps of fog like Triton's whore risen from the sea.

"I see," the *pizzella* says. She turns to me. "Fun and games. Too bad Turner came along."

"Most sorry," Turner says.

She turns now to him. "You might as well put that gun away. There are half a dozen police with me."

"Oh, of course. With John Wayne on his horse, leading the First Cavalry." He laughs. "Where are they, pray? Surrounding us? Preparing to sound the charge?"

"Looking for us," she says. "They'll find us eventually."

"Eventually."

"The more times you fire that gun, the quicker they'll find us."

"I needn't fire more than three times. Only once or twice, if you'll stand close together."

"You miss the point, Turner. The point is simply that I'm here. I was following you. There are police all around the lake, looking for you. Everyone knows you're here. So you can't possibly get away."

It began to penetrate. "What are you doing here?" he asked.

"I told you. Following you."

"Why?"

"You murdered your wife and Billy—"

"You can't know that! I have an alibi—"

"Sue me. I trusted Henry here." She shrugged apologetically. Cissy walked slowly to me and began to help me to my feet. "I'm a detective," the *pizzella* went on, "but also a woman. I applied police procedure and got nowhere. So I listened to my woman's intuition and I trusted Henry. It seems I was right." She glanced at me, standing naked in the dirt, leaning heavily on lovely naked Cissy. "*And* I was wrong," she said with a glower.

"It was all his fault," Turner said. "I had to kill Sarah because of him. He is filth."

"You can argue that in court," she said.

He laughed. "You must be as crazy as he is! You must think me insane. Or stupid. Come here."

"What?"

"Come here."

I started to move.

"Not you! You, Lieutenant Karen Douglass, you alone. Come here, to me. Slowly."

"Why?"

"Because you shall live. You have done nothing wrong, you should not die. And also," he added parenthetically, "it occurs to me that you might make a very effective hostage."

She shook her head. "It won't work."

"That's what they told the Wright Brothers. *Come here!* Now! Or I kill you all!"

She moved, one slow step at a time. The damned little idiot, she was a policewoman, didn't she have a gun? Does a trained police officer come chasing a killer halfway across the state without carrying even a dinky automatic?

Then I noticed her bag, under a tree where she'd dropped it when I knocked her down. The gun would be in there. Could I reach it?

I couldn't see how. Besides, I don't know how to fire a gun. Would it be on safety? What does that mean?

Nevertheless, I had to try. As she crossed the clearing toward Turner, I took my weight slowly from Cissy's arm and shifted it to my own two feet. . . .

I stumbled.

The shotgun swerved over and pointed at me.

I nearly collapsed. My right leg wouldn't take my weight.

I stood there on my left leg and stared at the shotgun leveled at me. I couldn't move. There was nothing I could do.

Nothing. A sheep in the slaughterhouse, waiting for the hammer.

"You can't escape," the *pizzella* was saying. "They won't let you go."

"They'll have no choice, with you along."

"Even if you get away, what then? Think of it. You're not in the Mafia, you have no organization to help you, no friends to run to. Are you going to exist as an outlaw? How? Robbing grocery stores for food? Where will you live? You can't go home—"

"Shut up! I'll worry about that later."

She was walking toward him. She was nearly up to him now. "You're giving yourself a life sentence," she said. "With no chance of parole. You'd be better off in jail—"

"Shut up," he said. "Turn around."

She did.

He came up behind her.

Curled his left arm around her neck, elbow tucked under her chin.

Rested the sawed-off barrel of the shotgun on her right shoulder, his finger on the trigger. Aimed at Cissy and me.

"All together now," he said, "repeat after me. 'Our Father, who art in heaven—'"

I pushed Cissy to one side, fell to the other, scrambled in the dirt for the bag with the gun—

He swiveled the gun on her shoulder and pointed it at me—I was stretched out on the ground, legs useless, hand stretching for the bag . . . helpless. . . .

His finger tightened on the trigger, the firing pin snapped—

She knocked the barrel of the gun up with her open palm as he fired.

Boom!

Stunned by the sound, stunned to be still alive, I lay on the ground and watched.

The shotgun had rested on her right shoulder, he was crouched over it as he fired. She extended her right arm and then brought it sharply back, slamming the point of her elbow into his gut. She stepped back with her right foot, placing it deep between his legs, reached up with her left hand and grabbed his jacket at the right shoulder, bent at the knees and slid her hip under his stomach and her right shoulder under his right armpit and then she straightened her legs and with her hip she lifted him off the ground, with her left hand she pulled him forward as she bent and straightened and twisted and she flung him over and through the air in a high arc, over her head and down she brought him, slamming him down on his back on the hard ground.

In the same motion the gun sailed out of his outstretched hand. She caught it in her right hand and slammed the wooden shoulder stock hard against his forehead, slamming his head back against the ground with all her might.

He didn't move.

He lay still.

Not a sound, not a twitch. He looked like he'd never move again.

And it was all over.

Just like that.

She bent quickly and undid his belt, pulled it away from his body. Unbuttoned his pants, unzipped his fly, pulled the pants down around his ankles. Rolled him over on his face, pulled his arms behind his back, wrapped and tied them securely with his belt.

Then she stood up, looked down at him, and with a deep breath and a long shudder relaxed. She walked over to Cissy and took a quick look at her arm. "Nasty," she said, "but not serious. It'll be painful when they dig the shot out, of course." She looked not uncheerful at the thought. She took off her jacket and helped Cissy into it. Cissy was shivering and her lips were blue. "You may be going into shock," Karen said. "Can you walk?"

Cissy nodded.

"Can you find our way to the cabin?"

She nodded. I stood up and limped over and took her arm.

"I'll help her, superhero," the *pizzella* said. "You carry my trophy." She gestured at Turner and put her arm around Cissy, and they moved off into the fog. I had a sudden urge to spank her.

I didn't think I'd better.

Instead I turned to Turner. I didn't see how I could carry him back, but I sure wasn't going to ask for help. Limping slowly, careful how I put my foot down, dragging him instead of carrying, somehow I made it.

Back in the cabin, I dumped him in a corner. He was conscious by now but didn't make a sound or a movement. He kept his eyes turned to the wall. My ankle and knee were beginning to swell, but I had feeling in both of them, at least. Nothing seemed broken or irreparably damaged. I wiped the blood off my backside, where the knife had cut me when I fell. It didn't look pretty, and it stung like hell when I washed it off, but it was a clean enough cut. It would heal. The rest of my body was a jagged series of scratches and little cuts. But nothing looked serious. I slipped into my clothes and started a fire while Karen wrapped Cissy in a blanket.

We huddled around the fire and I told the *pizzella* the whole story. "Where are all those policemen of yours?" I asked.

"They aren't," she said. "I was just trying to fuss Turner. Nobody in the department believed in my woman's intuition or in your instinctive understanding of Turner's mind. They believed his alibi. So I'm here on my own. But it doesn't matter now, does it? As soon as Cissy's feeling better, she and I will take the canoe into the village and call the police. And get her to a doctor. I assume you'll be able to manage Turner while we're gone?"

My knee and ankle were aching and puffy and the cut on my bottom had begun to bleed again and all the little scratches were beginning to itch, but I had the gun, he was tied securely, and he showed no sign of ever wanting to move again. I thought I might just be able to handle him for a few hours.

Handling *them* was something else again. I had no idea how I was going to do that. They sat there staring into the fire, Cissy huddled and thawing out in her blanket, the *pizzella* with her arm protectively around her. I had no idea how *that* was going to work out.

For some reason I thought of Damon and Pythias, Abélard and Héloïse, Beowulf and Lon Chaney.

Life is complicated, terribly complicated.

But interesting.